NICOLE

NICOLE

JACK WEYLAND

Deseret Book Company
Salt Lake City, Utah

Library of Congress Cataloging-in-Publication Data

Weyland, Jack, 1940–
Nicole / Jack Weyland.
p. cm.
Summary: Because he is attracted to Nicole Stegman, a musician in the pep band, Josh Dutton, high school basketball star, befriends her mentally handicapped brother, who helps Josh learn to see people differently just as Josh helps Nicole and her family renew their Mormon faith.
ISBN 0-87579-787-3
[1. Mormons—Fiction. 2. Christian life—Fiction. 3. Mentally handicapped—Fiction. 4. Brothers and sisters—Fiction.]
I. Title.
PZ7.W538Ni 1993
[Fic]—dc20 93-27303
CIP
AC

Printed in the United States of America

10 9 8 7 6 5 4 3

1

Josh Dutton opened the side door of the motel and started down the hall. A tall girl with a thick mane of brown hair came out of one of the rooms. "You're Josh Dutton," she said.

"Yeah, right. I guess you saw the game." Because he was the star of the Westmont High School basketball team, he was used to being approached by strangers. This girl looked familiar though. Coiled strands of brown hair cascaded down almost to the top button of her faded blue denim shirt. Her eyebrows were thick and dark and wide, as if a child had taken a crayon and scrawled a nearly straight, thick line over each eye.

"Yes, I was at the game," she said with little enthusiasm.

Josh was disappointed. Everybody else had told him what a great game he'd played; maybe she just needed a little prompting. "Well, what did you think?"

"I thought the pep band played great."

Josh wasn't used to being overlooked. Besides being naturally athletic, he had inherited his father's rugged good looks. "What about me?" he asked.

"You're not in the pep band."

"No, I'm on the team, and tonight I had twenty-seven points, eleven rebounds, and seven assists."

"Oh yeah? Hmmm . . . guess I wasn't paying that much attention. I'm in the pep band. We're kept pretty busy during a game, you know."

Josh decided two could play this game. "Let's see, the pep band? Oh sure, you're the group that kicks into action every time the ref has to wipe sweat off the floor. Gosh, what would we ever do without you guys?" With that he went down the hallway.

He found the soft-drink machine halfway down the hall. It had his favorite, Orange Crush. He was just about to drop his quarters in the slot when she wedged herself between him and the machine.

"Excuse me, but what are you doing here?" she asked. "I thought the team was staying across the street."

"Yeah, we are, but all the machines over there are empty, so I came over here to get something."

"Go someplace else."

"What for?"

"Because if I let you get away with it, then in five minutes the whole team'll come swarming over here, and before you know it, all our machines will be empty, and the pep band won't have anything to drink."

"Yeah, so what's your point?"

He noticed she spoke faster and more distinctly when she was mad. "My point is that just because you don't appreciate the pep band doesn't mean everyone else feels that way. Let me tell you something, we're important too. You try playing a game without us, and what've you got? I'll tell you what you've got. You've got ten sweaty guys with bony knees chasing a ball and smelling like bad cheese."

He moved in close to her face. "Is that right?"

"Yes, that's right."

They were less than six inches apart. He was six feet three; she looked to be about five feet ten. The light from the pop machine revealed a whole other world of hundreds of stray strands of hair. He imagined her hair to be an alien life-form with runners branching out to take over the world. She had the most beautiful jade-green "cat" eyes he had ever seen. They were so bewitching that he found it difficult to maintain eye contact and argue with her at the same time. So he shifted his gaze to her chin. "Look, I didn't come here to argue with you. Just let me get one can of Orange Crush and then I'll get out of here. And I promise I won't tell anyone where I got it."

"Sorry, but I can't let you do that."

He slammed the side of the pop machine with his open hand. "I can't believe this! I bust my back to win the semi-final game, and what thanks do I get from Miss Pep Band USA here? Nothing. Not even one lousy can of pop. Well, thanks a lot." He started back the way he had come.

She followed him down the hall. "Look, maybe I was a little too hard on you, but I'm sure you'll find something. I mean there's bound to be a 7–Eleven around here somewhere."

He could tell she was trying to smooth things over. He decided to take advantage of that, but first he needed to lull her into a sense of security. He stopped to let her catch up. "You know, I was just thinking, I was wrong to give you such a hard time. I mean, you were just sticking up for the pep band, and everybody knows they need all the help they can get. By the way, what's your name?"

"Nicole Stegman. We were in social studies together in ninth grade when you first moved here."

"Oh, sure. Sorry, Nicole, I knew you looked familiar." He flashed her his cheesiest smile. "Well, I'll remember you from now on. Yes, you can be sure of that."

They reached the end of the hallway. He pushed on the door as if he were leaving, then turned and ran full speed back down the hall toward the pop machine. He had the quarters he needed in his hand.

"Stop! I mean it too!" she called out.

He stopped and turned around. "Let me give you a little advice, Stegman. Never let your man get a step on you."

"You're very pleased with yourself, aren't you?"

"Why shouldn't I be? I outsmarted you. There's one thing you need to know about me, Stegman. I never lose. And I'm not about to start with you. I'll get what I came here for, and there's not a thing you can do to stop me."

"Is that right? Well, we'll see about that, won't we?"

"Who's going to stop me?" he asked.

"I'll stop you, Dutton. Anybody can see you're all bluff. The only reason you've got this far is 'cause you've never had any competition."

His mouth dropped open. Nobody talked to Josh Dutton like that.

They were glaring at each other as opponents when, by mistake, she let a silly little grin escape. She recovered fast but it was too late. Now he knew this was a game. More than anything, Josh loved games.

"Big talk, Stegman, mighty big talk," he said. "But the fact is, I'm about to walk out of here with an Orange Crush proudly in my hand."

"The only thing crushed when you leave will be your pride," she countered.

"Okay, Stegman, show me what you've got."

He could hear her giggling as they ran down the hall as fast as they could. He arrived first and dropped three quarters in the machine before she could knock them out of his hand. He punched the Orange Crush button, grabbed the can as it tumbled out, and waved it in front of her face. "What's this, huh?"

"Give me that can."

He obediently handed it to her, then turned and put

more quarters into the machine, retrieved another can, and gave that to her too.

She looked a little confused. "What are you doing?" she asked.

"Awarding you the coveted 'Trophy for Not Backing Down.' You are totally outrageous, you know that?" He spoke in his radio announcer voice. *"There she was, the Pep Band Kid, up against impossible odds, but did she back down? No, not her. Stegman does not know the meaning of fear.* Good job! Way to be! Man, this was great, wasn't it? You're good, you know that? You should've gone out for girls' basketball. Well, anyway, thanks. I had a lot of fun. And to think you come from the pep band."

He started down the hall backwards, talking to her as he headed toward the exit sign at the end of the hall. "Whataya say we do this again sometime? Your choice of hallways. Maybe after we get home after the tournament. Anyway, I'll see you around. Hey, give my best to the pep band. Really, I mean it. You guys are okay. I don't care what anyone says."

"Wait!" she called out. "Where are you going?"

He stopped. "Back to my room. Why?"

"You never got anything to drink."

He shrugged his shoulders. "Don't worry about it. Like my mom says, there's always water."

"Don't go," she called out.

He stopped. "Are you serious?"

She glanced around to make sure nobody had heard her. "I guess I could let you have one of these," she said, glancing down at the cans in her hands, "but only if you drink it here. And I'd have to be with you all the time to make sure you don't take it back to your room."

"Thanks, that'd be great. But I've got to sit down. I really got beat up out there tonight. Actually I'm one big bruise."

"There're some tables by the swimming pool," she said.

"No, it's too crowded. I don't want to talk to a lot of people. Let's look around, okay?"

In the basement they found a laundry room for motel guests; by that time of night it was empty. They sat down on the two red plastic chairs that faced a line of washers and dryers. A dog-eared copy of *Good Housekeeping* lay on a table in the corner of the room.

He took a big swig of Orange Crush. "By the way, Stegman, I've got to tell you this 'cause I've had to deal with it all night—you've got great eyes."

"They're the same ones I had in ninth grade. You didn't pay much attention to them then, so why the big interest now?"

"I'm a more sensitive and caring guy now than I used to be."

"Yeah, right, I'm sure that's it. Tell me something though—I'm curious. What's it like to walk down the halls at school knowing every girl is totally in love with you?"

"Actually I'm too busy to notice. I've got basketball practice until six every day. By the time I get home it's almost seven. I eat supper, do my homework, and go to bed. On weekends we have games. On Sunday I go to church. There's not much time left for anything else."

"Are you saying you never go out with anyone?"

"Well, not really. Last year I dated someone . . . strange girl though. She liked to eat butter sprinkled with sugar. One time I saw her eat a whole cube of butter. But then one night she just slipped out of my hands."

She smiled but at the same time shook her head. "That is so bad."

"Yeah, it kind of is, isn't it? I thought it was funny when I made it up—maybe not, huh? Oh well, it doesn't matter. We're having ourselves a good time, aren't we? At least I am. What about you?"

"Well, yes, I guess I am. To tell you the truth, I'm a little surprised. I figured all you'd want from a girl is for her to tell you over and over again how wonderful you are."

He played dumb athlete. "And that's bad, right?"

"How come you weren't this much fun in ninth grade?"

"Hey, I just played the best game of my life. Something like that tends to put you in a good mood."

"Were your parents at the game?"

"No, they couldn't be. My dad had to work tonight, but they'll be here tomorrow. My dad is the weatherman for Channel Three news. He goes by a different name for TV—Meteorologist Mike Kennedy."

"Oh, sure, we watch him all the time."

"My dad will appreciate knowing that. All my friends watch the Weather Girls on the other channel. What's your family like?" he asked.

"My dad has a construction company. I have a brother, too. His name is Richard. He's fourteen."

"I have an older sister. Her name is Kristen. She's on a mission for our church. We're Mormons."

"Actually I knew that," she said.

"What church do you go to?" Josh asked.

"We don't go to church anymore."

"You should go with me sometime." He finished his pop. "Well, that's the last of it."

"We'd better go. My roommates are going to be wondering what happened to me."

"Could we talk a little longer?" he asked. "I mean, you're not too tired, are you?"

"No, not really."

"Me neither. Why don't you let your roommates know you're okay and then come back here?"

"Ordinarily . . . " Her voice trailed off.

"I know. Me too. But this isn't an ordinary night, is it?"

"I'll be right back."

She returned a few minutes later. "My roommates hadn't even missed me."

"I did." He noticed she'd brought an instrument case. "What's that for?"

"You're such a show-off at games. I thought you should see what I'm good at."

"All right! We're going to have a concert."

A security man stuck his head in the door. He looked as if he were tired of chasing high school kids all over the building. "What are you two doing in here?" he asked.

"We're just talking," Josh said politely.

"You can't be here unless you're washing clothes."

"All right. Thank you, officer," Josh said. "Have a good night."

The security man, assured that Josh was not going to be a major problem, said good night and left.

Josh pulled off his sweatshirt and stuck it in one of the machines. "You got anything you want to wash? Like the man said, we can't be here unless we're doing laundry." Nicole removed her socks and dropped them in. He started the washer with quarters.

After closing the door and putting a mute in her trumpet, she began to play a difficult piece from memory. From the side, Josh noticed her face had a perfect profile. Not only that, but he had never heard a trumpet sound so good. When she finished, he gave her a standing ovation. "Man, that was great! Good job!"

"Thanks. It's for state solo competition. That's sort of the state basketball tournament for music."

"Hearing you play makes me wish I'd taken lessons."

She handed him the trumpet. "Want to give it a try?"

"Sure." He stood up and blew into the trumpet. It sounded like a sick moose. "Wow, pretty bad, huh?"

"No, actually that was good for the first time."

He blew into it again. "I'm sure I could get the hang of this."

"I'm sure you could too."

"Okay, I've got blowing down. Now show me how to work the buttons on top."

"They're called valves."

"Whatever."

She came behind him so she could work the valves with her right hand. He blew while she pushed the valves.

"You're doing really well," she said.

He gave her back the trumpet. "So are you. I'm serious. You're just what I need tonight . . . so I don't start getting uptight about the game tomorrow night."

She put the trumpet back in the case. "I never think of you being nervous. You don't show it during a game. Besides, you must like it, or you wouldn't keep doing it."

"I like it most of the time, but not before a game like the one tomorrow," he said.

"Look, it's very simple. You play to win, but if you can't win, then at least be valiant in the effort."

"That's good. Did you make that up?"

"No, it's something I've learned from my brother."

"I've got to meet this brother of yours. Okay, you've given me a trumpet lesson. How about if I show you how to play basketball? You've got good height and coordination. I'll bet you could really be good. I can teach you everything you need to know in about ten minutes." He opened the lid of the washing machine that wasn't being used. "Okay, this is the basket." He began speaking in his sports announcer voice. *"The game's tied . . . ten seconds to go. Stegman takes the inbound pass. She's heavily guarded."* He waved his hands in front of her face. *"She pivots . . .* Okay, pivot around. No, the other way. *She puts up a jump shot . . .* Okay, shoot . . . *It's good! Stegman has done it again! The crowd goes wild!"* He mimicked the sound of a cheering crowd. "Way to go! You carried the day!"

"Good for me. Does that mean I'm the hero of the school now?"

"Yeah, that's right."

"So, do I get to do the famous Josh Dutton victory swagger at school?"

"Sure, go for it."

She began chewing a big wad of imaginary gum and shuffled around the room imitating Josh. In as deep a voice as she could manage, she asked, "So, did you see the game? I had four thousand points, seventeen hundred assists, and six million rebounds."

"Gosh, you had a pretty good night then," he said.

She continued to imitate him. "Yeah, not bad for a superstar. There's one thing you've got to know about me, though. I never lose. Because I am a macho hunk. But sometimes a terrible thing happens—one of my teammates makes a basket without me. That's not good. Everything should focus on me. Me . . . me . . . me. That's what's important, and don't you ever forget it. I know I never do."

He was smiling because she imitated him so badly, but, even so, he still felt a mild rebuke in what she had said. "C'mon, Nicole, that's not fair. I'm not like that."

"Oh really? What about the game tonight? One of your teammates didn't pass the ball to you when you thought he should, so during the next time-out you went over to him and started yelling at him. I mean, there you are, telling him off in front of everybody."

"Yeah, well, that was in the third quarter. Eric Halbert didn't get the ball to me when I was open."

"And you don't think it's egotistical to act like you're the only one who can make a basket?"

"Look, you don't really know what you're talking about.

I was open. I had an easy shot. He should've got the ball to me."

"All right, fine, he messed up, but did you have to yell at him? I mean, he was doing his best."

"No, that's just it, he wasn't. Doing your best means you're thinking about what's going on out there. If he'd been thinking, he'd have got the ball to me and we would've had another basket."

"Another basket. That's all that matters to you, isn't it?"

He threw up his hands. "Are you serious? During a semifinal game for the state championship, yes, that's all that matters. All right, I admit it, okay? I'm a very competitive person. And I can't stand it when people don't perform up to their capabilities. Look, I don't want to complain, but a lot of times that's half our team."

"Except for you, right?"

"That's right. The coach says we've got to give a hundred and ten percent, and that's what I try to do. Is there something wrong with trying to do your best?"

"I don't know anything about basketball, okay? But I'll tell you one thing: watching you go after Eric the way you did made you look like a total jerk."

"Really?"

"Yes, really."

He shrugged his shoulders. "You know, I never thought about how it would look. Besides, I'm not out to impress people with how polite I am. But once a game is over, it's all forgotten. Eric knows that. He gets on my case sometimes too, so maybe it all works out."

"After the game did you tell him you were sorry?" she asked.

He shrugged his shoulders. "What for? We won, didn't we?"

"Would it be so awful for you to tell him you didn't mean it?"

"I did mean it. Face it, he messed up. I could've had an easy shot."

"So what? It wasn't that close a game."

"It doesn't matter. You've got to play every game like it's close. It's an attitude you've got to have if you want to be competitive. A hundred and ten percent in whatever you do."

She looked at him for a long time and then shook her head. "You know, it's amazing we're even talking to each other. We are so totally different."

"Yeah, we are. I like you though . . . sort of."

She crinkled up her nose. "Why? All I've done is put you down."

"Well, for one thing, you're a definite challenge. And for another, well, you're really good-looking."

"I suppose to someone like you, how a girl looks is the most important thing, isn't it?" she said.

"Excuse me, is this a trick question?"

"What I mean is, if you think about it, the way a person looks is really superficial."

"Maybe so, but let me tell you, the way you look is an Olympic medal kind of superficial."

They ended up looking into each other's eyes. He wanted to tell her how beautiful she was, but he was afraid she'd be threatened by that. He decided to buy time with nonthreatening conversation. "Tell me, do you prefer Nicole or Nikki?" he asked.

"Nicole," she said in a dreamy sort of voice.

Looking into her eyes reminded him of the first time he stood on the edge of the high-dive board and tried to build up enough courage to jump.

"Some people have nicknames, but others don't," he said.

"Yes, that's true," she said.

"A lot of people think my real name is Joshua, but it isn't. It's Josh."

"Really?"

Finally he had to state the obvious. "There is something going on here."

She shook her head. "No, I don't think so."

"I really like you," he said. He reached out to hold her hand.

It was the wrong thing to do. She got up to check on their clothes in the washing machine, then turned to face him. "Look, I've got to level with you. I'm not sure I trust you."

"Why not?"

"There're lots of reasons."

"Name one."

"Well, okay. At the game tonight one of the players on the other team barely touched you, and you fell backwards as if you'd been hit by a truck. Why did you do that?"

"I was trying to draw a foul. It worked, too."

"So you were faking it, right?"

"Sure. Why?"

"You're real good at faking things. Are you faking this?"

"Nicole, c'mon, that was a game."

"Yes, I know, but everything's a game to you, isn't it? Look, I have to go now. Let's just leave our things here. I'll put them in the dryer later tonight. You can pick up your sweatshirt tomorrow. I'll keep it in my room."

He carried her trumpet for her as they headed for her room. "I want to start seeing you after the tournament," he said.

"I don't think that's such a great idea."

"Why not?"

"I know this'll be a shock to you, but life doesn't revolve around basketball."

"I know that."

"You do?"

"Sure. In the spring there's track, in the fall there's football, and in the summer there's baseball."

"I'm talking about things that are important."

As much as he liked her, he was not about to cave in. "I am too."

They stopped in front of her room. "Well, thanks," she said. "I enjoyed getting to know you a little better. Now at least I won't be so quick to misjudge you. So, I'll see you around sometime, okay?"

She tried her key but a roommate heard her and opened the door and saw the two of them standing there. "Oh my gosh! It's Josh Dutton!" Two other girls suddenly joined her at the door.

"Good night," he said, aware of the spotlight he and Nicole had suddenly stepped into.

As he turned to leave, he could hear one of her roommates saying, "Okay, Nicole, you have to tell us everything that happened. And don't leave out anything either."

"Nothing happened," Nicole said.

He was still a little angry with her, so he decided to give her a hard time. For the benefit of her roommates, he turned around, flashed a big smile, and did his impression of a TV soap-opera leading man: *"Nicole, you've given me the most magical night of my life. Good night, my dearest."*

"You call that nothing?" a roommate cried out.

"Nothing happened," Nicole repeated.

"Oh, yeah, right. C'mon, tell us what happened."

He had almost reached the exit sign at the end of the hall when he heard someone running after him. He turned just as she reached him. Her jaws were clenched, her face red. "You can't help but play for the crowd, can you?" she said angrily. "You go back and tell the truth."

He followed her back to the room and poked his head in the door. "I was just kidding," he said. "Nothing happened between us. We talked, had some soda to drink, and that was it. We're probably not even going to see each other again."

"Fine, now get out of here," Nicole snapped.

"You shouldn't talk to Josh Dutton like that," one of her roommates said.

"I'll talk to him any way I want!" Nicole exploded as she slammed the door in his face.

A few minutes later, in the hall just outside his room in the motel across the street where the team was staying, Josh's coach caught him trying to sneak in. Because Josh had missed room check, the coach threatened to not play him for the championship game. Josh said he was sorry, and the coach finally relented and sent him to his room.

Josh could not remember having ever lost at anything. Tonight had been no exception.

Except, of course, for Nicole.

2

Josh woke up early the next morning. Even though it was the day of the championship game, his mind wasn't on basketball. He kept trying to figure out where he had gone wrong with Nicole. She was the only girl who had ever slammed a door in his face.

What's wrong with her anyway? he thought. *She has a totally unrealistic idea of competitive sports. She doesn't care how many points I make, as long as I'm polite. If I took her advice, we'd never win. The only way I know how to play is flat out. She thinks I'm overly critical of people's mistakes. Well, she's wrong—dead wrong.*

Because the shower spout was so low, he had to crouch down to get all of him wet at the same time. He wondered what idiot had designed the showers.

He knew he was hard to live with during a game. He demanded the best from himself and everyone else. There were times, though, when he wasn't out to win at any cost. For example, at church on Sundays. Maybe if Nicole knew about that part of his life, she wouldn't be so set against him. That's it, he would tell her about church. He decided to go see her.

Ordinarily he spent little time worrying about the way he looked. But that morning, as he got ready, he stared into the mirror and wondered if he had what it would take to interest a girl like Nicole. He was a little disappointed at what he saw because, more than anything, he looked like just another basketball player. His brown hair was cut short. He had a lean, chiseled jaw, and strong cheekbones that came partly from genetics and partly from running so much every day that it was practically impossible for him to put on weight.

Josh's mother was the one person who helped him understand who he was. She often told him what a great smile he had. Josh smiled in the mirror just to try it out. It didn't look too convincing. "Hi, Nicole, it's been a long time," he said, flashing a smile. He felt like he was practicing to become a greeter for Wal-Mart. He hoped none of his roommates were awake.

Basically he looked like a nice guy. That was a little disappointing, because for the first time in his life, he wanted more—much more. He wanted to send out invisible rays that would capture her heart and soul. He wanted her to cry out his name at night. He wanted her to beg him never to leave.

That's what he wanted. But staring at himself in the mirror made him think he wasn't going to get it. He needed some outside help to get the job done. He needed a secret weapon.

He needed aftershave.

But aftershave is not something ballplayers bring to a state tournament. He rummaged through his roommates' shaving kits. Nothing. He did find a fancy deodorant stick in one of the kits. He took off the top. He liked the smell, so he rubbed it on his face. At least it was better than nothing.

By the time he knocked on Nicole's door, it was eight-thirty in the morning. Nobody answered. He knocked several times before one of Nicole's roommates, wearing sweats as pajamas, came to the door. She was the girl who, the night before, had reminded Nicole not to talk mean to him. Even though he'd woken her up, she seemed glad to see him. "Hi, Josh," she said.

"Hi. Sorry it's so early."

"No problem. Oh, I'm Kim."

"Oh yeah. Hi, Kim. I need to talk to Nicole."

"Everybody's asleep."

"Yeah, I know. It won't take long."

"Sure, no problem." Josh thought Kim would go get Nicole, but instead she led him into the dimly lit room. Three girls were asleep in the two beds. "Nicole is the one closest to the window," Kim said.

Josh went to the lump next to the window and knelt down by the bed. "Nicole?" he said softly.

She opened her eyes, saw him, looked confused, and then panicked. "My gosh, what are you doing here?" She grabbed the covers and held them close to her as she sat up in bed.

"I couldn't sleep. I kept thinking about last night."

She brushed aside a few maverick strands of hair with her hand and glanced at the clock. "Is that really the time?" she asked.

"Yeah. Kind of early, right? Sorry."

She covered her mouth. "Oh man, I have pepperoni breath, don't I?"

"Don't worry about it. It's not that bad—really."

"We had pizza after you left. Who let you in?"

"Kim."

"Kim, why'd you let him in while everyone is still sleeping?"

"Because, well, he's Josh Dutton," Kim answered.

"What difference does that make?"

"Didn't you even watch the game last night?" Kim said. "If it weren't for Josh, we never would've won."

"So because of one game you think he should be able to come in here anytime night or day?"

"It wasn't because of just one game. Josh played great the whole season."

"I can't believe you, Kim. What if Mr. Peters catches him in here?"

The girl in bed next to Nicole rolled away from the noise. "Everyone be quiet," she moaned. "I'm trying to sleep."

"Josh Dutton is here," Kim announced proudly.

"I don't care." The girl pulled the pillow over her face.

"That's Trish," Kim said. "She's so sleepy, she doesn't even realize you're here."

"That's okay," Josh answered. Kim was really making him nervous.

"You can't stay here," Nicole said.

"I know. Get dressed and come to breakfast with me. There's a McDonald's not far from here."

"I told you last night I didn't think we should see each other again."

"And I don't blame you for feeling that way last night. I was still so pumped up about the game, I probably came across as a total jerk." He waited for her to say he hadn't come across as a jerk, but she didn't. He continued. "I never should have pulled that stunt with your roommates. I'm sorry about that. Look, give me another chance to show you I'm really not that bad of a guy. There're some things about me you don't know that will change your opinion about me. So come have breakfast with me."

"If you won't go with him, I will," Kim said eagerly. "In fact, I'll go take a shower now." She disappeared into the bathroom.

Nicole turned to Josh. "I hope you don't mind if I loan you to Kim."

"Yes, I do mind. She really makes me nervous. I don't

want to be with her. I want to be with you. C'mon, give me a break."

Strands of hair that had slipped back down in front of her face moved in the breeze of her prolonged sigh. "Oh, all right, but you'll have to give me some time to get ready. Go out in the hall and wait for me, okay?"

Nicole came out twenty minutes later and handed him his sweatshirt fresh from the dryer the night before. He put it on so he wouldn't have to carry it.

Once outside they could see the McDonald's sign three blocks away. It was a cold, windy March day. They hurried to get out of the wind. A few minutes later they sat at a corner table at McDonald's. She put her elbow on the table and rested her head in her hand while she yawned, then took a small bite of food.

"You okay?" he asked.

"Yeah, sure, I'm fine—just a little sleepy is all."

To him she seemed even more beautiful in the morning sunlight. He tried not to make her feel uncomfortable by staring at her as they ate, but it was nearly impossible. He stole as many glances as he thought he could get away with.

When she finished eating, she was all business. "You said you had something to tell me?" She grabbed a straw and bent it into three equal parts and connected the ends to make a triangle.

"I don't want to lose you," he said.

"Are you serious? How can you lose something you never had?"

"Well . . . I. . . . uh . . . "

"And another thing—how would you like it if someone compared you to something like a set of keys that can be lost or found or stolen? I don't belong to anybody and I never will. Nobody can lose me and nobody can find me. You got that?"

"Yeah, I guess so." Josh was frustrated. How could anyone make such a big deal out of "I don't want to lose you"?

"Okay, go ahead with what you were going to say," she said.

Now he wished he'd practiced in the mirror more. "I had the feeling last night that you might have been worried about, well, you know, what I had in mind, but the truth is, I wasn't even planning on trying to kiss you."

She closed her eyes and shook her head. "You're like a national treasure of totally inappropriate things for a guy to say to a girl."

"Sorry."

"I gave up sleep for this. So are you done? Because if you are . . . "

He wiped his forehead where sweat was starting to bead up. "I'm not finished. See, this first part was supposed to be like an introduction, you know, to sort of put your mind at ease."

"Oh yeah? It needs a lot of work."

"I know. This is really embarrassing. For some reason, when I'm with you, I can't seem to do anything right."

"Yes, I've noticed that. Why do you suppose that is?" She took another unused straw from the tray and bent it into a rectangle.

"I want us to be really good friends," he said.

"If you want a friend, try Kim. She's just what you need. Look, I can get her here in a couple of minutes. In fact, for all I know, she's probably hiding in the bushes somewhere outside just waiting for her big chance."

"I don't want to be with her. Well, okay, I'm ready to begin now." He paused to gather his thoughts. "I know you think I'm really selfish and only interested in sports, but there's a serious side to me you don't know anything about."

"Excuse me, I'll be right back." She got up, grabbed a

handful of straws, and returned to their table. The first thing she did was to blow a paper wrapper at him. It hit him on the nose. "Okay, tell me more about this serious side of yours."

He felt totally foolish. He had never opened himself up to a girl. "You only see me at games, but there's another part of me you probably haven't seen. I go to church every Sunday. I don't smoke or drink or use drugs. I try to be honest. I don't even watch R-rated movies. After I graduate, I plan on going to college for a year and then I'll go on a mission for my church for two years. Even now I go out once a month with this guy and, uh, we visit the homes of some people in our church, you know, to see how they're doing, and to try to help them if we can. What I'm trying to say is, I'm not as self-centered as you think I am."

She took the straw triangle and the rectangle she'd made and slowly pulled them apart and stuffed them in her empty milk carton. "Is that it? Are you done?" she asked.

"Yeah, I guess so."

She put her hand on his sleeve. "Josh, look, I don't want to hurt your feelings, but of all the things you could tell me about yourself that would make me want to stay clear of you, the fact you're a Mormon is probably number one."

He was in shock. "Why?"

"Nothing ever comes from arguing about religion, so let's not even get started, okay?"

"No, tell me."

"All right. The truth is that Mormons are hypocrites. They talk a good line, but they don't practice what they preach."

"How can you say that?" he asked. "You don't even know what you're talking about."

"I do though. See, the thing is, I used to be a Mormon."

"That can't be," he said.

"Oh, it's true all right. Our whole family was baptized when I was in the eighth grade. Not long before you moved here. Two missionaries going door-to-door found us. They taught us all about the church. They were okay, I guess. I liked the things they said. They promised a lot of things. They said it wouldn't matter to people in the church that my brother, Richard is developmentally disabled. They told us that the members were such good Christians that our family would always feel welcome at church. Well, it was a good sales pitch, but that's not the way it was after we joined."

"What happened?"

"Three months after we were baptized, we quit going because people were making fun of my brother while he was at church. We never went back. Nobody missed us that much. Really a great example of Christianity, right?"

"A lot of things have changed about the church since then. Even if your parents don't go, you should. Why don't you come to church with me sometime?"

Barely controlling her anger, she stood up. "I really have to go now," she said. She ran out of the building.

He caught up with her outside. "What did I say that was so awful?" he asked.

She had fire in her eyes. "You're absolutely certain I'm the one who needs to change, aren't you? Well, let me tell you something, there're a lot worse things than not going to church."

"Like what?"

"Like not caring about other people," she said.

"You mean people like your brother, don't you?"

"Yes, of course, that's what I mean."

"I don't have anything against your brother," he said.

"I know that, but I also know you'd be happy if people like him were kept away from you, so you never had to deal with them."

"It's just that when I'm around people like that, I don't know what to do," he said.

"So you don't do anything."

"That's right, but look—I can learn to do better. I know I can make friends with your brother."

"Do you think if you start saying hello to my brother, I'll be satisfied? You don't have the slightest idea what any of this is all about. Look, it's better if we don't see each other again. I know I'm hurting your feelings, and I feel bad about that."

They walked side by side with neither of them saying anything. By chance, his hand brushed against hers. The next thing he knew they were holding hands. They slowed down but kept walking. He knew that if he said anything at all, she'd pull away.

A few minutes later they stopped in front of her door.

"I'm sorry things didn't work out," she said.

"Yeah, me too. The church means a lot to me."

"I know it does."

"I'm sorry your family wasn't treated right at church. I wish I'd have been there. Maybe I could have made a difference."

"Things might have been different if Richard wasn't a special-needs kid. But he is."

"What if you and I and Richard did something together sometime?"

"I know you mean well, Josh, but really, give it up. It's hopeless."

"I don't agree."

"That's because in a game you never give up no matter how far you're behind. But this is different."

"Just give me a chance, that's all I'm asking."

For a brief moment she looked at him, and there was no bitterness or anger. It was more like it had been the night before. But then, like a tunnel caving in, it suddenly vanished again. "I hope things work out for you at the game tonight. I'll be cheering for you." She paused. "I mean it, Josh. It's my school too, you know."

The coach met with the team for two hours that morning and went over their game plan. After a large lunch, he told them to rest until the game. Josh and his roommates stayed in their rooms and watched TV all afternoon.

At two-thirty his parents called; they had just arrived in town. His father hadn't been able to come the night before because he had had to do the ten o'clock weather. And on Saturday morning he did a special weather report for children. Every Saturday morning he put on a rooster costume and presented "Willie the Rooster and His Wacky Weather Report." It was not something Josh bragged about.

His parents asked Coach Murillo for permission to spend some time with Josh before the game. The coach agreed.

Josh met them in the lobby of the motel. Ellis and Jeanine Dutton looked as if they were made for TV. Ellis, tall, velvet-voiced, handsome with his prematurely gray hair, was at home in any social situation. Because of his constant exposure on TV, people in the Westmont viewing area all felt as if they knew him. Jeanine Dutton, dark-eyed and slender, had been a great beauty when she was younger. Now in her late forties, she still caused heads to turn when she came into a room—but she maintained her figure only with ever-increasing efforts in aerobics classes.

Jeanine came from a wealthy family. In the beginning her parents were thrilled with their son-in-law, but now, after his being a TV weatherman in one small town after the other, they felt a little sorry for their daughter, especially when they made comparisons with their other children.

Ellis Dutton's income only provided for the essentials. Although the TV station he worked for covered hundreds of miles of farmland, its audience was relatively small, which meant that members of the news team were not paid anywhere near what they might have received in a metropolitan area.

Josh's grandparents had provided funds for Josh to attend BYU basketball camp during summers beginning the summer after he completed eighth grade. It was his grandparents who had made it possible for him to have a car during his senior year. It was also his grandfather's influence and money that had gotten him accepted into a prestigious private university in the East. Even his sister's mission was mostly being paid for by his grandparents.

Although he never admitted it, Josh was embarrassed by what his father did for a living. Right now in their hometown, there was a ratings war going on. His father was competing against the Channel Seven Weather Girls, three perky coeds from nearby State College. His father was a meteorologist who made his own forecasts; the Weather Girls smiled and joked their way through the forecasts they read from the National Weather Service. And yet more and more people were switching to the Weather Girls. Even Josh, in his own room, preferred watching them.

When Josh had been in fourth grade, he watched Willie the Rooster every Saturday morning. Now his only consolation was that none of his friends watched Willie and that only a few knew that Willie the Rooster was his father. The ones who did know, like his best friend, Kevin Buchanan, teased him about it.

Now, as they met in the motel lobby, Jeanine Dutton greeted Josh and said, "Your father has some good news."

"What, Dad?"

"It's not definite yet, but I got a call from the network yesterday."

"That's the network headquarters in New York City," Jeanine explained.

"They've seen some tapes I sent them of Willie the Rooster. They're thinking of using it nationally as a part of their Saturday morning programming."

"It would be seen everywhere," Jeanine added.

Josh had thought that when he went away to college, he would leave Willie behind once and for all. Even so, his father needed some kind of a break. "That's great, Dad," he said.

"Nothing's definite," Jeanine said, "so don't say anything to your friends."

"I won't. I promise." It was a promise he knew he would keep.

"Enough about me. How are you doing?" Ellis asked.

"I'm okay."

"Well, if you get nervous before the game, you might try those breathing exercises I taught you."

Josh felt bad about it, but lately for some reason, he discounted whatever his father said. His father, whose voice calmed people through blizzards and threats of tornadoes, was a strong advocate for using correct breathing in times of stress.

"And be sure to pray," Jeanine said. "Does the team have a prayer before the game?"

"No."

"They should. We always prayed when I was in high school, even before a basketball game."

"That was in Utah, Mom."

"It never hurts to pray," she said. "We could have a prayer here if you want."

Josh looked around the lobby. Some people had just come in. He could tell they were from Westmont because they recognized his father as their weatherman and were staring at them.

"No, I don't think so," he said.

Just before it was time for the team to travel by bus to

the university fieldhouse for the final game, the bravado Josh had tried to maintain for the benefit of his roommates had turned to nervousness. He decided to follow his mother's advice and pray. He made his way over the outstretched legs of his teammates, who were still sprawled in front of the TV in their room. Shutting and locking the bathroom door behind him, he knelt down, closed his eyes, and, in whispered tones, began. He asked that he wouldn't let everyone down, and that no matter how things turned out, the team would feel they had done their best. And then, because of the things Nicole had said about him, he added, "If you'll help me, I'll try not to be so selfish all the time. I'll even try to be a friend to Nicole's brother."

Someone knocked on the door. "Josh, it's time to go. You about done in there?"

Because Josh didn't want anyone to know he had been praying, he flushed the toilet. "I'll be right there."

He stood up. It was time to play basketball.

When the team went out onto the court to warm up, Josh felt as if someone had made a switch and given him an uncoordinated body. None of his muscles seemed to work the way they usually did. He had never played before such a large crowd before. He began the breathing exercises his father had taught him. As crazy as it may have appeared to his teammates, it seemed to help.

He looked in the stands for the pep band. For a second he made eye contact with Nicole. She smiled just as a ball passed from a teammate near the basket hit him on the shoulder. "Hey, wake up," one of his teammates said.

He had a slow start, but by the beginning of the second quarter he discovered a natural rhythm where everything he tried worked. It was as if nature had somehow conspired to give him this one perfect game to remember the rest of his life. He had never been one to make many three-point shots, but there was a period of time in the second quarter when he could not miss. He made five three-point shots in four minutes, one right after the other.

As the opposing team tried to keep him from shooting, passing opportunities opened up for him. He started to feed others for easy shots. By the time the second quarter ended, the score was 48 to 32. Josh had already made 22 points.

At the beginning of the third quarter, though, he twisted his ankle coming down on top of another player's shoes after making a layup. He ended up on the floor. The coach helped him back to the bench.

"I'm okay," Josh said.

"No, you're not. Sit down and rest."

Josh sat out the rest of the third quarter. He watched his team's lead shrink.

"We want the son of Willie the Rooster!" some guys called out. Josh turned around. Kevin Buchanan and the rest of the guys Josh ate lunch with were standing up and chanting.

A few minutes later Westmont trailed by two points. The coach came over to him. "How're you feeling?" he asked.

"I'm okay now."

"You sure?"

"I'm sure."

"Okay, I'm sending you in—but if there's any problem, I'm pulling you out."

Josh stood up and took a step. His ankle hurt when he put weight on it. He looked at the coach and forced himself to smile. "It feels a lot better now."

The coach wasn't fooled. "Yes, I can see that."

As Josh waited to go in, he said a silent prayer that he would at least be able to finish the rest of the game.

Neither team showed clear superiority in the fourth

quarter. They traded leads seven times. Although Josh was never able to get into quite the same rhythm he'd had earlier, he was still reasonably hot. Most of all, though, he was able to keep the other team intimidated enough to allow his teammates to be open more than they had been when he wasn't playing.

The game went down to the wire. Finally, with nine seconds left and the other team ahead by one point, Josh stole the ball, dribbled the length of the court, and made what turned out to be the winning layup.

Both teams were out of time-outs. The other team made their inbound pass to their best player, who dribbled across midcourt, threw up a desperation shot, and missed.

The game was over and Westmont had won 79 to 78. Josh was now under more danger from his own team members and fans than he had been from the opposing team. His best friend, Kevin Buchanan, a fullback on the Westmont football team, and several others came out of the stands and lifted Josh on their shoulders and carried him around the court. Josh had one hand in the air in a victory salute and the other hand on a shoulder of one of the boys carrying him. "We did it! We really did it!" he shouted over and over again, pumping his fist into the air.

Then he asked the boys to let him down so they could lift the coach up on their shoulders. On their way the coach got a bucket of water dumped on him, so that by the time they reached him, he was soaking wet. They lifted him up on their backs and paraded him around, but then one boy slipped on the water, and the coach, worried about safety, asked to be let down.

Somebody found a ladder and went to the basket and cut down the net as a souvenir. While everyone was watching that, Josh turned around and there were the cheerleaders. He hugged them all and then some other girls he didn't even know. After that there were two interviews with a TV news team and then the formal presentation of the trophy for being state champions.

In the locker room the shouting and celebrating went on all the time they were showering and getting dressed. Outside the locker room, after Josh had finished getting dressed, there were still people in the hallway wanting to shake his hand and take his picture and ask him about the game. A mother asked if he would pose for a picture with her ten-year-old son. He agreed. He even knelt down and talked to the boy. As he did so, he realized that a newspaper reporter was taking a picture of that too.

John spotted his parents near the back of the crowd and worked his way over to them. His mother gave him a big hug and exclaimed, "Oh, Josh, you did it! You really did it! I'm so proud of you!"

His father gave him a bear hug. "You were amazing out there, Josh. I've never seen you play better."

"Thanks, Dad."

"Look, that's the man who does the weather," a little boy from Westmont pointed out.

His father turned around as if they were on camera and smiled. "This is my son Josh."

Josh smiled into the imaginary camera too. *I'm becoming just like him,* he thought. It was a depressing idea.

The team bus didn't leave the fieldhouse until a little after eleven. They stopped for something to eat and then headed out onto the interstate. It was a four-hour trip across the state. At first everyone was fired up, but gradually, one by one, people fell asleep. Josh sat by the window and looked out at an occasional gas station or farm light. He found himself wondering why Nicole hadn't come to see him after the game and what she thought about him now.

3

There were two wards in Westmont. The ward Josh and his family belonged to met at one o'clock. That meant that Josh and his parents, who also had driven across the state that night, were able to sleep in. His father woke him up at eleven-thirty and told him it was time to get ready for church.

Josh got up and went into the bathroom. There, on the counter, laid out for him to see, was a page from the sports section of the newspaper. At the top of the page was a picture of him going up for a layup along with the headline "Dutton Sparks Westmont to State Title." The lead article told about the game. Further down the page was another picture of Josh, this one showing him talking to the boy he had greeted after the game. The article under this photo was headlined "Local Hoop Star Acts as Role Model." Josh read the article. It talked about his success in sports as well as some of his other accomplishments in high school.

A few minutes later Josh, now dressed for church, walked into the kitchen. His parents, who had already eaten, seemed to be waiting for him.

"A nice write-up in the paper today about you," his father said.

"It shouldn't have had so much in it about me. There're other people on the team besides me."

“I’m glad you feel that way,” his father said, “but I can understand why they wrote it up the way they did. People want heroes in their lives. They find them, for the most part, in sports. You were their hero last night. Next week it will be someone else. That’s just the way the media are.”

Just before church began, the bishop greeted Josh and asked him if he would say a few words in sacrament meeting. All through the first part of the meeting, Josh tried to decide what to say. After the sacrament was blessed and passed, the bishop called on him to speak.

Josh walked up to the stand and looked out across the congregation. There on the last row was Nicole Stegman, sitting all by herself. She must have come in late. Suddenly everything Josh had thought of saying seemed wrong. Because Nicole already suspected him of being conceited, he didn’t want to draw attention to himself.

“You don’t win a state championship all by yourself,” he began. “It takes a lot of people. We needed everyone, even the ones on the bench in case one of the starters got hurt. We needed the parents to support their sons who are on the team. I don’t want to take a lot of glory for what was a team effort, because that wouldn’t be right.”

After sacrament meeting Josh tried to reach Nicole to talk to her, but too many people wanted to talk to him. By the time he got back to where she had been sitting, she was gone.

During priesthood meeting Paul Baxter, who was in the elders quorum presidency, came up to him. “Are you too famous to go home teaching after you finish eating supper?” he asked.

“Not if Marilee has a treat after we’re done.” Marilee was Paul’s wife.

“How do chocolate chip cookies sound? She made them yesterday afternoon before we went to the game.”

"She's really great. How did you ever get her to marry you?"

"I just turned on the old charm," Paul said, knowing he was setting himself up.

"No, seriously, how did you do it? You had her parents kidnapped, right?"

Paul always had an easy smile. "Kids these days. Is six o'clock okay?"

"Yeah, sure."

"I'll come get you. As far as a lesson goes, maybe you could talk about what you learned about life during the tournament."

"Why, so it'd be less preparation for you?" Josh teased.

"I think we've been home teaching partners for too long. You know me too well."

"I like it that way." Josh was sincere; he really did enjoy being with Paul Baxter.

"Well, actually, so do I. My family feels the same way, Josh. We're proud to know you. Especially now that you've become a legend in your own time."

After supper Paul Baxter and Josh visited three families. Afterwards they went back to the Baxters' house for their home-teaching treat. Over the last two years Josh had learned a great deal about Paul and Marilee Baxter. He knew that, while attending college, Marilee had been on the Brigham Young University volleyball team. She loved sports and, even after two kids, still found time to keep in shape. The first time Josh ended up in their kitchen after having gone home teaching as Paul's companion, he wondered why she had married Paul. She was tall and beautiful, with a friendly personality, and people were always drawn to her. On the other hand, Paul could walk into a room and not be noticed. He didn't possess half the charisma that his wife had. They had met at BYU. Marilee once told Josh that the first thing she had been attracted to was

Paul's sense of humor, and the second thing was his strong sense of wanting to do what is right. Gradually he became her best friend.

The more time Josh spent with the Baxters, the more he could see that the combination of the two of them worked well. The thing he liked the most about being with them was that they could talk about almost anything. They never talked down to him or avoided difficult subjects or sugar-coated anything. He talked more freely with them than he ever would have dared to do with his own parents.

As usual, the three of them sat around the kitchen table and ate and talked. He told them all about Nicole.

"You say she and her family are in our ward?" Marilee asked.

"Yes, but none of them come anymore." He paused. "Except for today. Nicole came to sacrament meeting but then left right after it was over. The reason her family quit coming is because her brother is retarded. She told me they used to go to church but people made fun of him. So they quit coming."

"Why do you think she came today?" Paul asked.

"I don't know, except that maybe it's because I told her she should."

"You might be able to get her to start coming," Paul said.

"I don't think so. She's really down on the church."

"Do you like her?" Marilee asked.

"I guess so. That first time we were together, we had a really good time."

"So you two met at a tournament," Marilee said. "Very interesting. That's how I met Paul. It was a volleyball tournament at BYU. After one of the games, I came out of the locker room and there was Paul. He came up to me and asked for my autograph and told me he went to every home game and that I was one of his heroes. He was so nervous. He couldn't look directly at me either. And then he told me that he had my picture on his wall and that I was all he thought about, and he knew he was being silly, but could he have one of my sweat socks as a souvenir. And then he started blushing and told me he really liked my moves out there, especially when I jumped up and spiked the ball into the far court. And then he told me that if I would shake his hand, he would never wash it again. Well, naturally I didn't know what to say."

"Lies, all lies!" Paul interrupted her. "The reason she didn't know what to say is because this never happened. I didn't even know she was on the volleyball team until our third date."

"Don't listen to him, Josh. After that he kept calling me and pestering me to go out with him until finally, in a weak moment, I agreed. My life has never been the same since."

"You are such a con artist," Paul said.

"Who do you believe, Josh—the guy who drags you around visiting people till all hours of the night or the one who makes you chocolate chip cookies?"

"That's easy. I vote for the cookie lady."

"Yes!" Marilee said. "I flat-out beat you, Paul. When it comes to lying, I'm the best."

"I know. That's what worries me about you."

Josh looked at the clock. "I'd probably better get home now. I think I have some homework to do, but it seems like such a long time since I went to school, I can't even remember what classes I'm taking."

On his way home, he looked at his watch. It was nine-thirty. Tonight was Sunday. That meant his father, who got Saturday night and all day Sunday off, would be home. At ten he would watch the news and take notes, which he would review the next day with the weekend weatherman.

The Dutton family's schedule revolved around local news. Ellis was never home to eat supper with the family on weekdays. He was usually there in the mornings and early afternoons until it was time to go to the studio.

As Josh walked into his house a few minutes later, his father said hello and then commented, "You were gone a long time. Did it take that long to do your home teaching?"

"I went over and had chocolate chip cookies at the Baxters."

"Do you have your homework done?"

"Not really."

"Do you want me to call your teachers tomorrow and ask for a little more time?"

"No, that's okay, Dad. I'll take care of it."

"Are you handling fame okay?"

"Yeah, I think so."

"I think so too. I was impressed by what you said in sacrament meeting."

"Thanks, Dad."

Josh got ready for bed. At ten fifteen he went into the living room. His parents were watching the Weather Girls.

"What's the deal here?" Josh asked. "Checking out the competition?"

"Something like that," his father said.

"They don't know anything about weather or geography," his mother said. "The blonde just pointed to Iowa and called it Ohio."

Josh liked the blonde the best. "Hey, anybody can make a mistake," he said.

"I can't believe they let girls wear that on a local news show," his mother said.

Josh tried to add his support. "Maybe not very many people watch them," he said. "If I were a farmer and I needed to know what the weather was going to be, you know, like for planting, I'd sure as heck prefer finding out what the weather was going to be from Dad."

“Maybe so,” his father put in, “but the Weather Girls are hurting me in the ratings.”

“Yeah, but you can tell they don’t like weather as much as you do. When there’s a blizzard coming, nobody gets more excited about it than you. What we need is some really bad weather.”

During family prayer, Josh opened his eyes and stared at his father. He felt sorry for him. People at school talked about the Weather Girls all the time, but nobody talked about his father. This was more than just a slump. Josh used to look up to his father and wanted to be just like him, but not anymore. His father was stuck in a dead-end job. When Josh needed anything now, he didn’t even bother to ask his dad. He just called his grandparents. They always gave him what he asked for.

Josh hoped he didn’t end up like his father.

At school on Monday there was a pep assembly to honor the team. As the coach called out each name, a member of the team would walk out onto the gym floor while the students clapped and shouted and whistled. After everyone had been introduced, the coach said, “Josh Dutton is our team captain. He’d like to say a few words at this time.”

Josh walked to the microphone. “The guys wanted me to say a few words,” he began. “Mainly we just wanted to thank you guys for your support during the season. It was great all season, and especially at the tournament.” He glanced at a piece of paper on which he’d written a few notes. “Also, we want to thank Coach Murillo too. He always believed in us. Coach, the guys and I got together to get you something so you’d remember us after we’re gone. Guys, you want to bring it out?” Two team members brought out a gift-wrapped box and gave it to the coach. “Go ahead and open it,” Josh said.

As the coach opened the box, Josh said, "Okay, what it is, is a waffle maker. And the reason we're giving the coach that is because one of his favorite sayings is that life is like a waffle. You probably think that's a really dumb thing to say. Well, you're right, it is. I never wanted to tell you that before, Coach, but it really is." Everyone laughed. "But what are you going to do? He's our coach. If any of you guys want to know how life is like a waffle, just talk to any members of the team and we'll tell you. Anybody want to know? I didn't think so. We didn't either, actually. Well, anyway, Coach, thanks for a great season. Let's hear it for Coach Murillo!" Josh began clapping and the students joined in.

After the noise settled down again, Josh continued. "While I'm here, I'd like to say a couple of other things. You know, it takes a lot of people to make something like this happen. First of all, it takes all you guys coming to the games and showing your school spirit, and it takes the great job the cheerleaders did to keep everybody fired up. Let's hear it for the cheerleaders. Give me a C . . . "

Josh led a cheer for the cheerleaders, but by accident, he added an extra *E*. Once he realized his mistake, he added five extra letters, then ended with "What does it spell?"

Some in the audience tried to spell the letters. One of the cheerleaders stepped up to the microphone and tapped Josh on the shoulder. "It doesn't spell anything, Josh."

"Really?"

"Sorry."

Josh put his arm around her. "I never knew how tough it is to be a cheerleader. It's for sure I'd never make it, right? But, seriously, the cheerleaders have been a big part of the season for all of us. I just want 'em to know how much we appreciate all they do."

As the crowd applauded, one of the cheerleaders gave

Josh a kiss on the cheek. He leaned down to the microphone and said, "I love this game!" As usual, when it came to anything Josh did, the crowd loved it. He smiled at all the girls on the first few rows of bleachers and commented, "Well, I'm about done here—unless, of course, anybody else wants to give me a kiss."

Kevin Buchanan and another football player jumped up. "We do!" they yelled as they banged their way down the bleachers to the gym floor.

"Whoa! Stop! Forget it! I withdraw the offer!" The football players, looking disappointed, turned around and went back to their seats.

Josh pointed to the pep band. "Another group that doesn't get much thanks is our pep band. They really did a great job at the tournament. Could we have the members of the pep band stand up? Let's show 'em how much we appreciate 'em!" He got a good round of applause from the crowd.

Finally he concluded, "Right from the very first day of practice, this was a team effort. We set goals of what we wanted to accomplish this year. We worked hard all season to achieve our goals. Everyone worked hard to make it happen. I just want everybody to understand that. This has been a special year for all of us on the team. Thanks again. We love you guys. You're the best."

After the victory rally was over, Josh wanted to talk to Nicole, but she left before he could catch up with her. Because she had her trumpet with her, he figured she would be going to the band room to put it away, so he waited in the hall just outside the room.

When she came out, she seemed surprised to see him. "Hi, Josh."

"I thanked the pep band."

"Yes, you did. Thanks. I guess it's my turn. You really played well Saturday night. So once again you're the hero of the school, swaggering down the halls. So how is it for you this time?"

"It's embarrassing. I'm serious. Today everyone keeps staring at me. Like, if I want to blow my nose, I feel like I should go in a closet so nobody sees me."

"Are you saying that sometimes you have to blow your nose? Gosh, you've really let everyone down."

"Why didn't you come out to see me after the game?" he asked.

"What's the matter, didn't you have enough girls hanging on you?"

"You can never have too many. Besides, I wanted to talk to you."

"Josh, look, I thought we settled this already," she said, suddenly getting serious.

"I know, but you keep giving me mixed signals. On Saturday you said you didn't want to see me anymore, but then you let me hold your hand."

"I know. That was a mistake."

"And then yesterday you came to church. Why?"

"You asked me, remember?"

"What did you think?"

"I liked the things you said in your talk, but I didn't see anyone there like my brother. I don't think things have changed much since we quit going."

He paused a moment, then said, "I want to meet your brother."

"Why?"

"I don't know. I just do, that's all."

"All right, maybe sometime you and I and Richard could do something together. We could have lunch at McDonald's. Richard likes that."

"How about this Saturday?" he asked.

"Okay, but I still don't know why you want to do this."

"You're the one who told me I was too wrapped up in myself."

"I also told you that you couldn't have any Orange Crush. You didn't pay attention to me on that, so why should you on this?"

"Before the game on Saturday night I promised somebody I'd get to know Richard better," he replied.

"I was the only one talking to you about that, wasn't I?" she asked.

"Yes."

"So who did you make this promise to?"

Josh realized he had said too much. "What difference does it make?"

"I just want to know, that's all." She thought about it, then said, "Oh, my gosh. It was God, wasn't it? You said a prayer before the game, didn't you!"

His face turned bright red. "Don't make fun of this."

"I'm not making fun of it. I just never imagined you had any depth to you, that's all."

"Most of the time I don't," he said.

They stopped talking and stared into each other's eyes, unaware of people brushing past them on their way to class.

"What am I ever going to do with you?" she asked.

"Let me be a part of your life."

"You wouldn't be comfortable there."

"Let me be the judge of that."

"Josh, right after the game I did want to come and see you," she confessed.

"Why didn't you?"

"I don't know. I should have, I guess."

"I thought about you all the way home," he said.

"I thought about you too." She paused. "But I still say this isn't a good idea."

"I love your eyes . . . "

"Josh, don't."

The class bell rang. Neither of them moved. "You got a class to go to, mister?" she said, sounding like an army drill sergeant.

"Yes, sir," he answered, saluting her.

"Then you get there right away or else show me your hall pass. What you're doing right now is totally unacceptable behavior for an educational institution."

"Your eyes . . . "

"Go to class. I mean it!"

"Yes, ma'am." He started to walk backwards.

"Josh," she called out.

"What?"

"If it's too awful for you on Saturday and you really can't handle being with Richard, just tell me, okay? I'll understand."

"All right, fair enough. See you around, okay?"

That night he looked through last year's school annual and cut out a picture of Nicole. It wasn't a good picture; the photographer had caught her blinking. And because it was in black and white, it didn't do justice to her eyes or the sassy smile she gave him sometimes.

He didn't expect her to be much fun until after he had met her brother. For some reason, everything seemed to depend on that.

4

On Saturday morning, a little before noon, Josh drove slowly by the address Nicole had given him. It was an old two-story house. The vacant lot next to it must have belonged to her family too, because it was filled with equipment her father used in his construction business—a snow-scraping blade that attached to a pickup truck, a Bobcat tractor for small outside work, a black flatbed truck used for hauling lumber, scrap lumber of various sizes and lengths, and a junked-out car. In the driveway was a pale blue Ford pickup with a Stegman Construction sign on the door and the motto, "We make your dreams come true." The garage was built for two cars but was filled with more equipment and supplies. It didn't look as if a car had made it inside the garage for years.

Because Josh had grown up in a house where things were always put away, he was a little critical of the clutter. He wasn't sure what he was getting himself into. He made a U-turn and pulled up in front of the house. The front door was open except for the screen door. As he walked up on the porch, he could see Nicole vacuuming the living room carpet. He rang the bell but she couldn't hear him.

A minute later she turned off the vacuum cleaner and called out, "Mom, is Richard dressed yet? Josh'll be here any minute."

"I thought you were trying to hurry him up," a woman's voice called back from another room.

"I was, but when I came into the living room, I saw he'd spilled his Cheerios in front of the TV, so I had to clean it up. I want the house to look clean for Josh."

"I guess he'll just have to take us the way we are."

"What's this, a boy is coming here for Nicole?" her father called out from another room. "Looks like I need to get out on the front steps and clean my rifle. Who is this boy anyway?"

"Josh Dutton. We spent some time together at the state tournament."

"Is he the one Kim was talking about?" her mother asked. "The one who came to your room when everyone was still asleep in bed?"

"Whoa! Run that by me again," her father called out. "How come nobody ever tells me these things?"

"Because you always overreact," Nicole's mother said.

"Who's overreacting? I'll just break this punk's arm when he shows up, that's all."

Suddenly Nicole turned and saw Josh at the door. She hurried over. "How long have you been standing there?" she asked.

"I just got here," he lied.

"Come in." She called out to her parents, "He's here!"

"Where's my rifle?" her father yelled.

"Don't mind my dad," she said, inviting Josh in. "He likes to tease. Oh, this is my mom."

As Carol Stegman walked into the room, Josh noticed that she had no-fuss short dark brown hair and was at least three inches shorter than Nicole. The term "Super-Mom" came to his mind. His own mother had always made sure he and his sister were cared for, but she had outside interests that kept her busy as well—aerobics, church callings, serving on the city library board of volunteers, singing in a community choir that practiced once a week. Nicole's mother, on the other hand, devoted all of her time to her family. This was not a woman who spent hours getting her hair fixed or leisurely shopping for the right dress to wear to a community event.

"Josh, it's great to finally meet you," she said, reaching out to shake his hand. "I've heard so many good things about you from Nicole."

"No kidding. Sometime when she's out of the room, could you tell me what she said about me?"

"Anytime."

"Hey, wait a minute," Nicole protested. "Josh is in our house five seconds, and already you two are plotting against me?"

"Absolutely. You don't stand a chance," her mother said. "Look, Josh, we're kind of in a mess today, so you'll have to bear with us. But it's not all bad news. I made some sticky buns for breakfast. Would you care for one or two with some milk?"

"Sure."

"C'mon in the kitchen then," she said cheerfully.

"I'm going to see what Richard's doing," Nicole said. "Would you mind keeping Josh company till I get back?" She began walking up the stairs while her mother and Josh went into the kitchen.

"I'll take care of him," her mother called after her. "Here, Josh, let me clear a place for you. Please excuse the mess. My husband's in the construction business. Our kitchen has always been too small, so for years I've been after him to put an addition on the house so we could have a dining room. Last October he finally framed it in, but he hasn't done much else on it since then. Today he's putting up Sheetrock. Right now there's a lot of clutter, but it'll look a lot better by suppertime. So for me this is a happy day."

She set a glass of milk and a plate with two sticky buns in front of him at the table.

He took a bite. It tasted heavenly. "Oh, my gosh, this is so good!" he said.

"I bake every Saturday morning. You're welcome to come around anytime you want. I take 'em out of the oven about nine o'clock."

"My mom never bakes things like this. She and my dad are always on a diet."

"I should be, but life is complicated enough around here without me trying to starve myself too."

"I agree. You just keep making these things and I'll be over here every Saturday from now on," Josh said.

"Okay, it's a deal."

Nicole came downstairs. "Richard decided to take a shower," she explained. "I told him not to but he went ahead anyway, so it'll be a few more minutes. Sorry."

"I don't mind," Josh said. "I'm having a good time. Your mom's a great cook."

Nicole sat down while he finished eating. Then she asked, "You want to meet my dad?"

"Yeah, sure."

"Okay. Well, I'd better warn you—he really likes to tease. And sometimes he can look like he's serious when he's really just joking, so keep that in mind. Take my hand, and I'll lead you through the maze."

The new dining area had two entrances, one leading into the living room and the other into the kitchen. Since the doorway connecting to the kitchen was blocked with construction materials, she led him through the living room.

"Now there're saws and tools everywhere so be careful, okay?" she warned him.

Dave Stegman, a big man with a crew-cut hair style, was wearing jeans and an old plaid shirt. He looked up as they came into the room and Nicole said, "Dad, this is Josh Dutton."

Dave looked Josh over and then, with a teasing grin, said, "Definitely time to clean my rifle."

"Dad, shush."

Dave walked over to Josh and observed, "He's tall and strong. Very good."

"I told you he was on the basketball team," Nicole explained.

"I used to be quite a basketball player in my time," Dave said.

"Did you play on a high school team?" Josh asked.

"Well, no, not exactly. It was just a bunch of guys."

"I'm going upstairs to check on Richard," Nicole said. "I'll be right back. Dad, can I leave Josh with you? You won't embarrass him, will you?"

"Me? How could you even think that? Josh and me'll have tea and crumpets and talk about the weather."

"I'll be just a second. Now, Dad, you remember what you promised. When I get back I'm going to ask Josh to tell me everything you said to him, okay?"

"You worry too much."

Ten seconds after Nicole left, Dave Stegman had forgotten his promise. "So what were you doing in my daughter's motel room in the middle of the night?" he asked.

Josh decided Dave Stegman was the kind of father he wanted to be if he had daughters. He felt a little intimidated by the question, but he was not about to give the man the pleasure of watching him squirm. "Say, you think we'll get any rain here anytime soon?" he said, ignoring the question.

"Good answer. You're going to fit in around here just fine," Dave said, laughing.

"Thanks. Oh, just for your information, it wasn't in the middle of the night. It was a little before nine in the morning."

"Well, you've got to understand that to Nicole, that is the middle of the night. I don't think she's ever seen a sunrise."

"And the reason I went there was to ask her to go to breakfast."

"And did she?" Dave asked.

"Yes, she did."

"She always did have good sense. I think she got that from me."

"That's pretty obvious," Josh said.

"How about handing me that hammer?"

When Josh gave him the hammer, Dave asked, "Can you use one of these?"

"Well, yeah, I guess so. Probably not as good as you can though."

Dave smiled. "Probably not. Want some practice?"

"I guess so."

"How long are you going to be out with Nicole and Richard today?"

"Two or three hours, I guess," Josh said.

"When you get back, you want to give me a hand? It's a lot easier to put Sheetrock up with two people helping out. Hey, but if you can't, that's all right. I can get my wife to help me. Or course, her back has been bothering her lately, but, hey, we'll get by. Don't worry about us."

Josh was pretty sure Dave was running a scam on him about his wife's back, but he didn't mind. "I'll help," he said.

"Terrific. That'll give us a chance to get to know each other better."

In an upstairs bedroom, Josh could hear Nicole pleading, "Richard, we've got to hurry. Now try and remember, when's the last time you saw your shoes?"

"Tuesday," Richard said.

"Today is Saturday. I know you had them on yesterday.

C'mon, Richard, help me look for them. Josh is here. We need to go. . . . Oh, here they are. Put them on. Now, Richard, you've got to promise to behave when we're in McDonald's, okay?"

"Okay." There was the sound of shoes clunking down the stairs, and then Nicole's fourteen-year-old brother entered the room. His plastic frame glasses were taped in at least three places and perched on his nose at an angle. His brown hair was neat in front, but it stuck straight up in the back. He had a noticeable gap between his two front teeth. He was only a couple of inches shorter than Nicole but looked as if he would make that up before very long.

"Well, here we are," Nicole said. "We're all ready. Richard, this is Josh. He's the best high school basketball player in the state."

"The best basketball player in the state?" Richard asked, wide-eyed.

"Yes. When there're only a few seconds left in a game, he can grab the ball and run to the other end and make a basket. Not only that, but he's a very good runner in track and he played on the football team too."

Richard came over to Josh and with great enthusiasm said, "Thank you for coming to our house."

"Here, Richard, this will show you how good he is." Nicole showed him the newspaper clipping of Josh going up for the winning basket.

"This is you?" Richard said after looking at the picture.

"Yes, it's me," Josh replied.

"You were in the newspaper?"

"Yes."

"You must be famous. Thank you for coming here!" Richard threw his arms around Josh and gave him a big hug.

"Richard likes to hug," Nicole said. "I hope you don't mind."

Josh assured her he didn't mind at all. Then Richard dropped to the floor and undid one of Josh's shoes.

"What are you doing?" Nicole asked.

"I want to see his feet."

"No, Richard . . . "

"It's okay," Josh said. He sat down and let Richard take his shoes off.

Richard touched each toe gently and then on an impulse pulled off his shoes and socks and compared his feet with Josh's. "His feet are longer," he said.

"Yes, but he's older," Nicole told him. "Your feet will be his size when you're his age."

Josh glanced up as Carol Stegman entered the room. They made eye contact, and he sensed that she was there to make sure her son was treated fairly.

"Josh runs like the wind," Nicole told Richard.

"I want to run like the wind. Can you teach me?"

"Sure, if you want me to," Josh responded.

"I do. Stay here tonight. We have a TV. You can watch it, if you want."

"Everyone has a TV, Richard," Nicole said.

"Dogs don't."

"That's right. Dogs don't, but Josh isn't a dog."

Richard laughed and petted Josh's head. "Nice doggie. If you stay here tonight, you can sleep in my bed."

"No, Richard, Josh has a bed of his own," Nicole said.

"He can sleep in your bed then."

Nicole shook her head. "We've talked about this before, Richard. Nobody sleeps in my bed except me."

"I did once."

"That was when you were little and there was lightning and you were afraid. Josh isn't staying the night with us, but do you want to go out for a lunch at McDonald's with him and me?"

"Yes! Let's go!" Richard headed for Josh's car.

Once they were in line at McDonald's, Josh turned to Nicole and asked, "What would he like to drink?"

She put a hand on each of his cheeks and turned his face so he was looking at Richard. "He's right here. If you want to know what he wants to drink, ask him yourself."

"Sorry."

"That's all right. Everyone does it."

While they stood in line to order, someone left the door into the cooking area open. Before they could stop him, Richard was in the kitchen. They could hear him saying, "Hello, how are you? My name is Richard. What's your name? Do you like cooking? I want a hamburger. Is that my hamburger you're cooking? How can you tell which hamburger is mine and which is my sister's? How do you keep track of everything? I've never been in here before. My sister has a boyfriend. He's the best basketball player in the state. He wants a Big Mac and fries and a Sprite . . . "

"You'd better go get him," Nicole said.

"Will you go? I need to stay here and order."

She smiled. "Sorry, but this is your service project, not mine. You go. I'll order. Just make sure you're back in time to pay for it."

Josh coaxed Richard out of the kitchen and got him to stand in line, but while they were waiting for their food, he slipped away again. By the time Josh was paying for their order, he could hear Richard in the dining area: "Hello, my name is Richard. How are you? What's your name? What is that you're eating? Can I have some? Thank you very much."

"Richard, you shouldn't be bothering people when they're eating," Josh said, walking over to get Richard.

"I'm not bothering them. They like me. Everyone, this is Josh. He's my sister Nicole's boyfriend. He's the best basketball player in the state. He's going to stay at our house with my sister tonight."

Josh's face was turning red. "Richard," he said, "I'm not going to stay overnight. You need to sit down so you're not bothering people."

"I don't bother people. I'm just friendly."

They moved as far away as they could from the people Richard had been bothering and sat down. Richard seemed incapable of sitting still. After a few bites, he got up and was gone again.

"It's your turn," Josh told Nicole.

"No, it's your service project," she countered.

"You're enjoying watching him run me around, aren't you?"

She smiled. "Yes, I am, actually." She paused. "Look, if you want, we can take our food to a park and eat there."

"Yes, let's do that."

They drove to a park that served as a flood plain to the river that wound its way through Westmont. It was an overcast day with the temperature in the mid-fifties. They ate on the swings. Richard stayed put only while he ate and then he was off again on another adventure, this time with the monkey bars.

"Look at me!" he said as he climbed to the top.

"Yes, Richard, that's real good, you're on the very top," Nicole called out.

"You didn't seem embarrassed at the way Richard was acting at McDonald's," Josh said to Nicole.

"Why should I have been? He was just being Richard. That doesn't bother me." She paused. "What bothers me is when people call him a retard, or when they treat him like he can't do anything, or when all they can see are the bad things. There are a lot of really wonderful things about him. He gives the best hugs. Whenever I come home, he lets me know he's glad to see me."

"I told some friends at church he was retarded. Is that what I should have said?"

"I say that he's developmentally disabled. Retarded really sounds bad."

"Does he go to a special school?" Josh asked.

"No. He has some classes, like chorus and art, in a regular class, but with classes like English, he meets in a small group with a special ed teacher."

"Let's walk to the dam and feed the ducks," Richard called out as he headed up the bike path that ran alongside a river.

"C'mon, slowpoke, see if you can catch me," Nicole said to Josh, as she began running after Richard.

"Of course I can catch you," Josh called out. "Besides being the best basketball player in the state, I'm also the fastest runner."

She stopped running and turned around to face him. "Yeah, right."

"I'm serious. I took first in the 800-meter race at state last spring."

She flashed him an impish grin. "That's only because you weren't racing me."

"Oh, I see. This is like at the motel, is it? Well, I beat you then and I'll beat you now."

"Big talk. Face it, Dutton, you're a wimp," she said. They took off running. They ran past Richard, who was cheering for Josh. Just before Josh caught up with Nicole, she raised her hands in triumph. "I won!"

"No way."

"I won! See, the finish line was here!" She pointed to a rock just behind her.

"What a convenient finish line."

She flashed a big smile. "Yes, isn't it?"

Richard caught up with them. "Josh was the winner," he said. "Josh always wins."

"See there?" Josh said. "Richard knows who's the best."

"All right, I give up. You won."

They continued walking up the bike path. Richard kept running ahead of them and then coming back. "Don't tire yourself out, Richard," Nicole warned.

"I'm not tired."

"You're not tired now, but remember—we have to walk back to the car too."

Five minutes later they reached the dam and the shallow lake behind it. They stood on the lakeshore and tossed stones into the water. Josh looked for smooth flat stones, and Nicole coached Richard on how to throw them so they would skip across the surface of the water. After a few tries he finally got one to skip three times.

"That's the record!" Nicole cried out.

"All right, Richard, you did it!" Josh cheered.

Richard plopped down on top of a picnic table. "Let's look at the clouds!"

They lay down next to him and looked up. They told each other what the shapes reminded them of. Then Richard got up to go throw more rocks into the lake.

Josh sat up, and Nicole scooted next to him. "How's this been for you today?" she asked him.

"Better than I thought it would be. I actually think it's been good for me."

"In what way?"

"I never realized how busy I've been. I never get a chance to look up and watch the clouds go by. Basketball is over, but now there's track to worry about. Once actual meets begin, I'll be tied up every Friday until school's over."

"Look at me," Richard called out. "I'm skipping rocks!"

"Good job, Richard!" Josh called back to him.

"We'd better go see what he's doing," Nicole said.

They found a bench to sit on where they would have a clear view of Richard on the shore throwing rocks into the lake.

"This is working out great," Josh said. "You watch Richard and I'll watch you."

"Stop," she said.

"What?"

"You're embarrassing me."

"I can't help it."

Suddenly they heard a large splash and looked over to where Richard had been standing. He had either jumped or fallen into the lake. Josh ran down to the shore and into the water, grabbed him, and pulled him onto the bank. They were both wet and covered with mud.

"Cold!" Richard gasped.

"Is he okay?" Nicole asked.

"Yeah, he's fine, but can you go get the car?" Josh asked. "We'll start walking down the bike path, but I think you'll make it faster than we will." He dug the keys out of his jeans pocket and tossed them to her. She ran along the path back to the car.

"C'mon, Richard, let's go as fast as we can. The sooner we get to the car, the sooner we'll be warm again."

They made slow progress. Richard was miserable, and no amount of coaxing would convince him that hurrying would make things better.

A short time later Josh was glad to see Nicole driving his car up the bike path, honking at a biker and two joggers to let them know she was coming.

Josh had Richard sit in the front passenger seat so he'd be near the heater, and he climbed into the back seat. He told Nicole to drive to his house because it was just a few blocks from the lake. When they arrived, they hurried inside. Nobody was home. Josh took Richard into the bathroom and had him undress and get into a shower to warm up. Then he showed Nicole where things were in the kitchen and asked her to heat up some soup.

Richard's shower seemed to last forever. He started

"Not now. I have to jump to the top of that tree."

"Richard, if we don't go now, we'll get in trouble," Nicole said.

It took a while to talk Richard off the trampoline, but finally they managed to do so and went in the house.

"Mom, Dad, this is Richard and Nicole," Josh said.

Richard took one look at Josh's father and exclaimed, "Hey, I know you! What are you doing here?"

"I live here."

"You live here?"

"I'm Josh's father."

"That is so wonderful! Josh, did you know that your father is on TV?"

"I knew that, Richard."

Richard looked at Josh's mother and asked, "Who are you?"

"I'm Josh's mother."

"But who else are you? Are you on TV too?"

"No, two celebrities in a family are enough."

Richard, without any warning, threw his arms around Jeanine Dutton. "Thank you for being Josh's mother. He saved my life, and did you know he's the best basketball player in the state? Also, I've seen him in his underwear."

"Not another word, Richard. I mean it too," Nicole said, quietly.

"Do you want to tell him about Willie the Rooster?" Josh's father asked Josh.

It was the last thing Josh wanted to bring up to anybody. "I don't think so, Dad. If we tell him, we'll never get out of here. Maybe later though, okay?"

When they arrived at her home, Nicole told her parents what had happened at the lake.

"You sort of specialize in being a hero, don't you?" Dave Stegman said to Josh.

"Not really."

"I suppose after saving somebody's life, you're probably too tired to help me put up Sheetrock, right?"

"No, I can help. That's why I'm here."

"That's great. Nicole, either help us or get out of the way. I don't want you distracting Josh. He's working for free. I want to get my money's worth."

"I'll help," Nicole said.

"Somehow I knew you would. Okay, let's go to work. We've got to be finished by six."

"Why six?" Nicole asked.

"Because that's when your mom's going to feed us."

They worked hard and fast. The hardest part was putting up Sheetrock on the ceiling. Josh had to hold it in place while Dave nailed it up, and by the time they were half done, his arms were aching.

"How you doing?" Dave asked. "You want to take a break?"

"No problem."

"What a guy," Dave said, smiling. "I feel fine too," he added. "Of course, I won't be able to feed myself tomorrow, but, hey, that's okay, right? I know you don't need a break because you're a man of steel, and, of course, I don't either, but let's take one anyway, okay?"

They went into the kitchen and had the last of the sticky buns and something to drink. Richard came into the kitchen and asked, "Josh, do you want to see my medals from Special Olympics?"

"Sure, why not?"

"Come with me then."

Richard led Josh upstairs to his bedroom and took the medallions and ribbons from a nail on the wall. As he held up each one, he read on the back what it was for and then draped it around Josh's neck. There were ten medals in all.

"I've never known anyone with so many medals, Richard," Josh told him. "You've really done great."

"I'm a winner."

"Yes, you are. I can see that."

"And now you're a winner too because you're wearing my medals," Richard added.

"I'm wearing them, but I didn't earn them. You did. Thanks for letting me see them. It's a great honor. Here, I'll give them back. I need to get back and help your dad some more."

They finished their work at five-thirty. "You learn fast, Josh," Dave said. "If you ever want a job, let me know. I can put you to work anytime."

"I might take you up on that sometime. It was really kind of fun."

"You like my daughter enough that you might be coming back next weekend? The reason I ask is, I need to do some taping and texturing."

"Sure, I'll help. Next Saturday, right?"

"Yes, unless you want to do it tomorrow."

"No, I'll be in church tomorrow."

"All day?"

"No, but I'd rather not work on Sunday."

"Church, huh? I guess that's okay for some people."

"Would you mind if Richard went to church with Nicole and me?"

"You can't change the world, Josh," Dave said. "You can't make everything right." He stopped, then apologized. "I'm sorry. You don't know that yet, do you? You'll find it out soon enough."

"I guess I don't know what you're talking about."

"You think you can take Richard to church and everyone will treat him right, don't you? We thought so too once, but it didn't work out, so we quit going. Did Nicole tell you what finally made us quit? Someone told my wife that there must be some other place where Richard could go to church where he'd fit in more and wouldn't disrupt their meetings so much. That did it. We never went back. Nobody ever came to tell us they missed us either. Of course, I knew they wouldn't. And that was the end of it for us. Give it up, Josh, and stick to something easy, like putting up the winning shot in a championship basketball game."

5

On Wednesday Josh was invited to have supper with Nicole's family. Nicole greeted him at the door and invited him in. Dave Stegman came into the living room, where they were sitting, and said, "It looks like supper will be another half hour. You want to take a ride with me so I can show you some of the things we've built over the past few years?"

"Yeah, sure."

"Nicole, we'll let you come too."

The three of them got in his construction company pickup and took off. They drove a couple of blocks and stopped. "See that house?" Dave pointed to a house on the other side of the street. "I built that two years ago."

"And it's still standing today," Nicole teased.

"The things we build stay built. I check back with all my old customers and make sure everything is okay. You make people feel good about what you've done for 'em, and they talk to their friends, and that brings more business." He drove to the next block and stopped. "We put an addition on that house last summer," he said.

"Dad, if we're going to visit every place where you ever pounded a nail, we'll never eat," Nicole pointed out.

"Okay, okay, just one more."

They drove past a restaurant. "We did the remodeling

on that place before it opened up as a restaurant," Dave explained. "Used to be a grocery store. Even today we can drop by anytime and the owner stops whatever he's doing to fuss over us. He lets us pick whatever we want from the menu, and it doesn't cost us a cent. That's what having happy customers is all about. There's one other place just around the next corner . . . "

"This isn't fair," Nicole interrupted him. "On Saturday you forced us to work without any breaks, and now you're trying to starve us to death. You don't treat the people who regularly work for you this bad."

"Well, yeah, I know, but you're family."

"Josh isn't."

"You never know. He might be someday."

"I can't believe that you said that. Josh and I are just friends," she protested.

"And that's the way it should be. But Josh, if you ever end up being my son-in-law, just think of all the fun we'll have. Every weekend we'll be adding on to my house. I'll end up living in a mansion and you'll end up with a bad back. Sounds great, huh? Man, there's nothing I like better than free labor, and that's the truth."

"Thanks for the warning," Josh commented.

"But it wouldn't be all work. There'd be some good things about being in the family. You'd get to be with my daughter anytime you weren't helping me."

"Dad, that's enough, and I mean it!"

"You're right. I never know when to stop."

Eating supper with the Stegman family was like watching a three-ring circus.

"Do you like tomatoes?" Richard asked Josh, his voice louder than anyone else's.

"Yes, I do, Richard. How about you?"

"I like tomatoes. Especially the small ones you can put in your mouth and bite down and they shoot all over."

"Would you like some more salad?" Carol Stegman asked.

"I ate a green tomato once. It was yucky," Richard said.

"No, thank you," Josh told Carol.

"Are you sure? We have plenty," she said.

Richard continued talking. "One time we picked all the tomatoes from the vines and that night it froze everything."

"What I want to know is how you two got together," Dave Stegman said.

"We wrapped the tomatoes in newspaper and put them in a box, and then when we needed tomatoes we just went and got them," Richard went on.

Josh began to answer Dave's question. "All the drink machines on our floor were empty so I went over to the motel across the street to get me something to drink from one of their machines," he said. "Nicole saw me and said I couldn't have any. She was worried the rest of the team would come over and empty their machine."

"She wouldn't let you get anything?" Dave asked, sounding surprised. "Nicole, you've never told us this part of the story. This is very interesting."

"Do you like tomatoes on hamburgers, Josh?" Richard asked.

"Yes, I do."

"Me too."

Just before dessert, Dave noticed that Richard had not eaten his lima beans. "Richard, finish up your lima beans so you can have dessert," he warned.

"I hate lima beans," Richard said.

"There's not that many. If you don't eat 'em, you can't have any dessert."

"I'm not eating them."

"Richard, don't create such a disturbance with Josh here," Dave said.

"I'm not creating a disturbance," Richard said. "I just don't like lima beans."

"Beans are good for you," Nicole said.

Richard grimaced. "They're not good for me. They're bad for me."

"They're good for everyone," Nicole said. She put a lima bean in her mouth and commented, "Look, I like them . . . ummm good."

Richard smiled. "If you like them, you can have mine too."

"Just try one bean . . . for me," Nicole said. "Okay?"

"Just one bean?"

"Just one bean for me."

Richard put a bean in his mouth, chewed it, then spit it into his napkin.

"You didn't swallow it. That's not fair."

"One bean, one bean, one bean, that's what you said! One bean, you said, and one bean I did."

"Richard, stop it," their father said, his voice rising. "Your mother has worked hard to fix this supper, and it's not fair for you to refuse to eat it. You won't get any dessert and you won't leave this table until you finish your lima beans."

"I'll stay here forever then, because I'm not eating them, not ever, not in a million hundred years."

"It's up to you, Richard."

Nicole took up the role of peacemaker. "Dad, maybe it does taste bad to Richard. We don't know how his sense of taste is. It might not be the same as ours."

"He's got to learn that there are some things in life you have to do even if you don't want to do them. I want him to eat his lima beans. And don't you go eating them for him. We've got to teach him to try to cooperate before he gets out of control."

The rest of them finished their dessert, and then Dave

said he needed to go give a home owner an estimate on a remodeling job. Carol also excused herself and went upstairs.

"Richard, would you like an orange shake?" Nicole asked.

"Oh yes, I love them!" he said enthusiastically. Then, because his mother had pounded it into him, he added, "But no sugar."

"I know just how to make it yummy for you," Nicole said. Josh followed her over to the kitchen counter, where she plunked ice cubes into the blender, added orange juice, and then, without Richard seeing her, dumped the lima beans from his plate into the blender.

"Why can't he have sugar?" Josh whispered.

"Every time he has some, he ends up with seizures all night," Nicole answered. "He's allergic to milk too." She poured the mixture into a glass mug and took it over to Richard, then sat down to watch him drink it.

"You're so good to me," he said, taking a big swallow. "But Dad is mean."

"He's not mean, he just wants us to—"

"—eat our beans," he said, finishing her sentence.

She smiled. "Yes, that's right, he just wants us to eat our beans."

"Beans, beans, the musical fruit," he chanted.

"Yes, Richard, that's right."

"How long do I have to stay here?" he asked.

"Just until you finish your drink."

His face lit up. "Just until then? You mean I don't have to eat my lima beans?"

"Nope, not as long as you finish your drink," Nicole said.

He leaned over and hugged her. "You're so good to me."

"That's 'cause I love you."

"I love you too, Nicole, a million hundred times."

In the Stegmans' driveway was an old basketball hoop and backboard nailed to the garage. After Richard finished his shake, Josh talked him and Nicole into going out and shooting baskets. They played until it got too dark to see; then he went home.

After saying good night to his mother, he went to his room and turned on the TV just as his father began the weather on Channel Three. He switched to Channel Seven so he could watch the Weather Girls.

The next week Ellis Dutton flew to New York to meet with some television network executives about the possibility of a national audience for his Saturday morning weather report.

"Did he take his rooster costume with him?" Josh asked his mother in an unguarded moment.

"I won't have you speak about your father in that tone of voice. Who do you think you are anyway?"

Josh was surprised. His mother hardly ever got mad at him.

"I'd think you'd be proud of your father for even being considered by the network for their Saturday morning programming," she said.

"My dad and Teenage Mutant Ninja Turtles. What a combination."

"You listen to me, young man. Your father gets hundreds of letters a year from children who love what he does."

"But they're not actually writing to Dad. They're writing to a rooster."

"And you're ashamed of that?" she asked.

"Yes, I guess I am, a little. I mean, at least Nicole's dad builds things that last. Mine just says if it's going to rain or not, and half the time he's wrong about that."

"What are you afraid of, that your father will be a success and will end up on national TV? Or that he won't?"

"I don't know. I just know I don't want to be like him, that's all."

"That's strange, because every day I pray that you will. He loves what he does and he's good at it. He's a wonderful husband and father. What's so terrible about that?"

"Nothing, I guess. Sorry." Josh knew it was no use to argue. His father was good at what he did, but what he did could be done as well by the Channel Seven Weather Girls. Announcing the weather didn't require a person with a master's degree in meteorology. Josh promised himself that when he was the same age as his father, he would be financially able to provide for his children's education and missions, and he wouldn't need his wife to ask her parents for a handout every time they needed money. He decided that Nicole's dad was more like what he wanted to be someday.

The first time Josh kissed Nicole was the next Monday at the free-throw line on an empty basketball court in the high school gym. He had worked that afternoon on a basketball clinic for seventh and eighth grade boys. His coach had asked him to help out; there was some pay for it also. They worked with the boys from four to six-thirty.

Nicole showed up around six to watch. She sat high up in the bleachers and worked on her homework. Occasionally she looked up, especially when she heard Josh's voice.

At six-thirty the session was over. A few of the boys seemed to take forever in the shower. Coach Murillo asked Josh to stay behind until everyone had left and then lock up. Finally, by seven o'clock the last of the boys had gone and the gym was empty.

"Hey, you up there!" Josh called to Nicole up in the bleachers. "You have to leave now. I'm locking up."

She slammed her book shut. "I hate to leave, you know what I mean," she said, speaking in her version of a male athlete. "Sports is my life." She started down the bleachers.

"Oh, really? I didn't know that," Josh said.

"Oh yeah, you kidding?" She continued her imitation of an athlete. "To me there's nothing sweeter than a slam dunk." She reached the gym floor and started toward him. "Slam dunks are my life. Too bad it's so late—I could show you some great moves."

"It's not too late," he said. "Show me what you got." He tossed her the ball.

She held the ball in her hand and walked directly toward him. They met at the free-throw line.

"You traveled," he said.

"Hey, nobody's perfect."

There was no mistaking the romantic tension between them. They were moving closer together, not touching, looking into each other's eyes. "So, where're all those great moves you were bragging about?" he asked. "You come up and stare at me. Is that the best you can do?"

"It's good enough to bring you to your knees."

"This isn't fair," he said.

"Why not?"

"It just isn't."

She still held the basketball. It stood between their getting any closer.

"Get rid of the ball," he said.

She let it drop and roll away.

He put his arms around her and kissed her.

"Wow," he whispered in her ear.

"Wow yourself."

"I think I have your face memorized," he said. "I'll prove it to you too. Here, I'll close my eyes." He reached out until the tips of his fingers were resting on her cheeks. "Okay, these are the cheeks I love to touch." He gently moved his fingertips across her face. "And these are the lips I love to kiss." He ran the tip of his index finger over her lips.

"And these are the teeth that are about to bite your finger off unless you quit messing with my face," she warned.

He smiled, dropped his hands to her shoulders, and hugged her. "I wish we could go on like this forever," he said.

"Me too."

They were just standing there with their arms wrapped around each other. His face was lost somewhere between her earlobes and her hair. He wondered if it was her perfume or her shampoo that smelled so good.

"What time is it?" she asked.

"It's not forever yet."

A minute or two passed, during which time they kissed once more.

"We need to keep track of the time," she said.

"Why? If I tell you the time, you'll say it's late and you need to get home."

"But it is late—and I do need to get home."

"Yeah, I know. Me too. We'll go in a minute." He reached out and took her hand. "This isn't just another game with me," he said.

She glanced around the gym. "Funny you should say that here."

"I'm serious."

"Good. It isn't just another game for me either, Josh."

They walked to his car in a daze.

The next morning he picked her up and drove her to school.

"Josh, I saw how good you were with those kids yesterday," she said. "Is that something you enjoy?"

"Well, yeah, I do. I was thinking that someday I might want to be a coach."

"You'd be a good one." She paused, then said, "What would you think about coming with Richard when he goes to Special Olympics practice? You might like that too. I know they could use you."

"Sure, why not?"

After school on Wednesday Josh went with Nicole and Richard to the weekly Special Olympics practice at a local park. Nicole introduced him to Brandy Wilson, the Special Olympics coach. Brandy, who was in her early thirties, was slender and of medium height, with short brown hair and freckles. She had the raspy voice of a chain smoker; it was a voice that could move mountains.

The first thing Nicole did was to make sure Brandy knew how good Josh was in basketball and track. She even showed her the tournament clipping from the newspaper.

"You here just to watch, or is it okay if I put you to work?" Brandy asked him.

"Put me to work," he said.

"Can you run a stopwatch?"

"Sure can."

"Good. I'll have you record the times. Nicole, can you try to keep peace among the troops?"

"All right."

"Anything you want to know about Special Olympics in Westmont?" Brandy asked. "We started with three kids. Now we're up to twenty-five. Not bad, huh?"

"Brandy is great with the kids," Nicole explained to Josh.

"Sometimes I think about giving it up, but deep down I know I can't," Brandy said. "It sort of takes over your life after a while. It'll happen to you if you stick around long enough."

One by one each of the Special Olympics team members arrived. When they were all there, Brandy called them together and asked them to sit on some bleachers behind home plate of the baseball field adjoining the track.

"All right, listen up," she shouted. "Yo, Larry! Keep your hands to yourself."

"He started it."

"I don't care who started it, keep your hands to yourself. All right now, we're a team now. We have to act like a team. You can't be mean anymore. What's your question?"

"Are we going to have uniforms?"

"Yes, we're going to have uniforms. I'm working on uniforms. Derek, sit down. You have to sit down for this part. The rest of us are sitting down."

"I can't sit down anymore," Derek said.

"Why not?"

"I have to go to the bathroom."

"All right, you know where it is, right? It's that small building over there. Do you know which door to go into?"

"Yes."

"Don't say yes if you're not sure. Are you sure?"

"Sure. It's the one not wearing a dress," he said, referring to the symbols on the door.

"Okay, hurry right back. Chris, sit on your hands. You heard me, put your hands on the bench. Okay, now sit on them. Larry, sit down. We're almost done."

"I have to go to the bathroom too."

"You can go after Derek gets back," Brandy said.

"It'll take too long."

"He'll be back soon. Gina, quit picking at your face. Okay, listen to me, everyone. This is Josh. Have you all met him?"

"I have."

"That's good," Brandy said.

"I have."

"Just raise your hands if you've met Josh. Chris, you're not raising your hand. Didn't you meet Josh?"

"You told me to sit on my hands."

Brandy suppressed a smile. "Oh, right. Did you meet Josh?"

"Yes, but I don't like him."

"Why don't you like him?"

"Because he doesn't like me."

"Josh, is it true that you don't like Chris?" Brandy asked.

"No. I like you, Chris," Josh said.

"Do you like me?" rang out a ragged chorus from everyone else.

"I like you all."

"Listen up now," Brandy said. "Josh is the best high school basketball player in the state, and last spring he was the fastest runner in the state. He's come here to help us run fast."

"He can run like the wind," Richard said proudly. "And he loves me."

"Do you love me?" a chorus of voices asked.

"I love Richard because I know him real well, but I'm going to love all of you as soon as I get to know you."

Several minutes later Derek came back from the rest room looking dejected.

"Derek, did you have a problem?" Brandy asked.

"The door wouldn't open."

"It's not open? It's got to be open. Josh, will you go with Derek to the rest room?"

"Sure. C'mon, Derek, let's go."

Josh found that the door was not locked, but the doorknob was hard to turn.

Once the practice actually began, he timed each of the team members as they ran fifty yards. He called out each time and wrote it down on a clipboard Brandy provided for him. Somewhere during the practice he began to realize that individually these kids would always be singled out as being slow or below average. But when they were together, it didn't make any difference. He had gone through high school listening to Coach Murillo encourage team members to give one hundred and ten percent, and he could see that Special Olympics team members could also give that kind of effort.

When he took Nicole and Richard home, Carol Stegman invited him to stay for supper. After supper the three of them ended up again in the driveway, shooting hoops. They played until eight-thirty, when Richard was called in to get ready for bed.

With Richard gone, Josh and Nicole had a shooting contest. She wasn't very good, but Josh appreciated the fact that she never gave up and also that she wasn't afraid to get a little sweaty. He loved to watch her move. His enjoyment had very little to do with basketball.

After several tries she made a shot. She turned around and flashed him a broad grin. "All right, Dutton, the pressure's on," she said. "Think you're up to the challenge?"

"Hey, anybody can get lucky." He shot the ball and it rippled the net cleanly. He turned and gave her his most arrogant smile.

She scoffed. "Like you said, anybody can get lucky."

"Except with me it's not luck."

"I know. With you it's a miracle," she said.

"Oh, is that right?"

"Yes, that's right."

She was just about to shoot again when he came behind her and nudged her elbow. The ball didn't even hit the backboard, thudding instead against the garage door. She turned around and began moving toward him. "Intentional foul. You're out of the game, mister."

"I didn't foul you," he protested.

She kept coming at him. "Don't give me that. It was a deliberate foul. That means I won the game."

She was very close. "You know what?" he asked. "When I look at you, I get weak in the knees."

She thought about that and then a big smile crept across her face. "All right!" She kissed him, then grabbed the ball, turned, went in for a shot off the backboard, which she made, and turned around with her own version of a cocky smile. "Never let your guard down, Dutton. That's the first rule of basketball."

"And what's the second rule of basketball?"

"I haven't got that far yet."

"You're not much of a coach."

"Never said I was."

He dribbled toward her, pivoted around, and drove in for a layup.

"Let's take a break and get something to drink, okay?" she said. They went inside and sat at the kitchen table and had some grape juice.

"Josh, tomorrow night is our spring band concert," she said. "I've got a couple of solos. Will you come to it?"

"Yeah, sure, if you want me to."

"I know you probably would never go by yourself, but it'd mean a lot to me if you were there."

"No problem."

"Thanks."

"What'd you think about Special Olympics today?" she asked.

"It was a lot of fun. I think I'll ask my track coach if it'd be all right if I missed the first hour of track practice every Wednesday so I can help out."

"You think he'll let you?"

"I think so. I usually get what I want."

For some reason that set her off. "No conceit in your family—you've got it all, right?"

"That's not being conceited, that's just being honest."

"You get what you want, right? Does us starting to kiss fall in the category of another of Josh Dutton's victories?"

He sensed an edge in her voice. "This is a trick question, isn't it?" he said.

"I guess that depends on your answer."

He was clueless. "Give me a hint—what am I supposed to say?"

"You might try just telling the truth."

"Sounds risky. The first time we were together, I wondered what it would be like to kiss you."

"So you set a goal and then worked to achieve it, right? Just like you do everything else in your life. Did you have a game plan for me too? Josh Dutton—state champion basketball star, track ace, and just recently on kissing terms with Nicole Stegman."

"I can tell you're getting mad at me, but I'm not sure why."

"There's a lot of talk about the guys you run around with, about the way they treat the girls they go out with. They go for as much as they can get and then brag about it afterwards. I know they're your friends, so I can't help but wonder if you're at all like them."

"Has any girl ever said I was like that?"

"No."

"That ought to tell you something."

"I don't want you talking to Kevin, and those other animals you eat lunch with, about us. I don't want to find out you've been talking about me like you talk about one of your great moves in a game. If I find out you've done that, then you and I are history."

"It'll never happen, so don't worry."

6

Josh's best friend in school since his family moved to Westmont had always been Kevin Buchanan. Both of them played on the school football and basketball teams, but as they had grown up, Josh grew tall while Kevin got big. In his senior year as the starting fullback for their team, Kevin had set a school record for most yards gained during a season.

Kevin and Josh always ate together along with four or five other athletes. For the most part girls stayed away, except to stop by and say hello on their way out of the cafeteria. Occasionally a girl might be invited to sit with them, but because the talk was often harsh or cruel or sexist or about sports, no girl lasted more than two days. Even girls who were going with some of the guys in the group stayed away and waited to see what they could salvage of a normal relationship after lunch.

Josh was the only Mormon in the group. He knew there were some rough edges to his friends' remarks, and at times he had to tell one or another of them that he didn't appreciate what they'd said. But still they were his best friends. He had always taken for granted his place in the group. It was his power base.

At lunch on Thursday, Kevin told him that it was the birthday of one of the cheerleaders, and some of her friends were going to throw her a surprise party that night. "Why don't you come too?"

"Yeah, sure, no problem," Josh said. Then he remembered the band concert Nicole had invited him to. "Oh, on second thought, sorry, I won't be able to go."

"Why not?" Kevin asked.

"I have something else I need to go to."

"What?"

"Well, actually, the band concert," Josh said.

His friends howled. "The band concert? Since when do you go to band concerts?" Kevin asked.

"I can go to a band concert if I want."

"It's that fox you met at state tournament, isn't it? She's in the band, isn't she?"

"Yeah, right, she plays the trumpet."

"The trumpet, huh? Well, I bet her lips are in good shape," Kevin said.

"No comment," Josh replied, with a big grin.

"So why are you going to her concert?" Kevin asked.

"She asked me to."

"She asked you to? What's happening to you? Look, if you start doing everything she asks, you'll end up canning fruit and taking out the garbage. Be a man. Let her know who's boss."

"Yeah," someone else said, "don't let her call the shots. Skip the concert and go with us."

Josh argued, but in the end he let himself be talked into skipping the concert. *After all,* he thought, *I don't like band music anyway, and besides, these are my friends. I can't let them down.*

And so Josh missed Nicole's concert.

When he woke up the next morning, he felt guilty. He waited in the hall for Nicole to get out of her third-period class. When she came out, she glanced at him and kept walking. Her stare had been so cold, it scared him away from even trying to catch up to her.

During lunch he tried to get advice from his friends. "I think Nicole is really mad at me for not going to her concert," he explained.

"She'll get over it," Kevin said. "Just leave her alone for a few days. Whatever you do, don't admit you were wrong. She's the one who has to learn to live with you. She's got to know who's boss. She'll come around in a few days."

"What if she doesn't?"

Kevin shrugged his shoulders. "Hey, it's no great loss. There's always someone else you can take to the free-throw line."

Josh turned red. "How do you know about that?"

"One of the janitors saw you two," Kevin said. "He told Eric yesterday, and Eric started spreading it, so by now it's all over the school. You two are famous. But why should I be surprised? You've always done well at the free-throw line."

After track practice Josh called Nicole. She hung up on him.

The next day he caught up with her at her locker. "Excuse me, I'm in a hurry," she said.

"Okay, I admit I should have gone to your concert. I'm sorry. Something came up at the last minute."

"Don't lie to me. I know where you were."

"All right, I was with some of my friends. What's so bad about that?"

"You said you'd go to the concert, and then, when something better came along, you didn't even have the decency to tell me you'd changed your mind. There's no excuse for that, Josh. None at all."

"All right, I'm sorry."

"Sorry? Sorry doesn't even begin to cover it. And another thing, why did you tell everyone about what happened in the gym that night?"

"I didn't tell anyone. One of the janitors saw us. That's how it got out. It wasn't me."

"I don't believe that," she said. "I don't believe anything you say anymore."

"I said I was sorry, didn't I?"

She slammed her locker door shut and stormed away.

He caught up with her. "I'm still going to work with Special Olympics," he said. "I've got permission from the coach to miss the first hour of practice once a week."

"Make sure they put your picture in the paper."

"I thought you'd be happy I'm going to help out."

"You do what you want, Josh, but of course I'm sure you will. You always do what you want and you always get what you want. That's just the way it is with you, isn't it?"

"I really am sorry for missing the concert."

"You should be, because that was my last concert. It's over, and no matter how many times you tell me you're sorry, I'll always know you really didn't really care about me. I can't even begin to tell you how angry I am about this. If you had a sick relative or if there'd been an emergency, I could understand that, but I know what you did that night. You went to Tiffany Branson's birthday party, and you sat around with all your macho friends and told them everything about us."

"I didn't talk about us."

"I think you're lying. And if you think you're the kind of guy I want to spend time with, then you're more of a fool than I thought you were. Stay away from me. I mean it, Josh." She brushed his shoulder as she walked away.

The next time Josh saw Richard was the following week at Special Olympics practice. He could tell by the hurt expression in Richard's eyes that he knew there were problems between Josh and Nicole. She had driven Richard to practice and then stayed in her car and did homework while she waited.

Near the end of practice, Richard walked up to Josh. "You were mean to Nicole," he said.

"I know. I'm really sorry about it, too."

"She went into her room and closed the door. I think she cried."

"What can I do to make it better?"

"Tell her you're sorry," Richard said.

"I already did, but it didn't do any good."

"I'll help you tell her then. Come with me."

Richard went over to the car, with Josh a few steps behind. "Josh says he's sorry," he explained to Nicole.

"Richard, get in the car," she said. "We need to get home."

"Josh, tell her."

"I'm sorry I hurt your feelings," Josh said.

"Richard, get in the car," Nicole repeated.

"He said he's sorry, so you've got to forgive him," Richard said.

"He says a lot of things."

Richard grabbed Nicole's hand and then Josh's hand and brought their hands together until they were resting on top of each other. Then he put his own hand on top of theirs so they wouldn't pull away.

"Please give me another chance," Josh said.

"You got to now," Richard told her. "Josh didn't mean to hurt you. So will you? Please, for me and for Josh, please, with sugar on it. Please say yes."

She got out of the car. "I'll talk to him, Richard, that's all I can promise."

Richard came in close to hear what they would say. She turned to him and said, "We need to be alone for a minute, Richard, okay? Please wait in the car."

She and Josh walked a short distance away. For a moment she looked him without speaking. Then she said, "Before we can even think about starting over, I want you to see the videotape of my concert."

After taking Richard home, they picked up the video and went to Josh's house so they could watch it without being distracted by Richard. It was a painful experience for Josh because, after each number, she stopped the tape to tell him what she had been thinking at that point in the concert.

"Before the concert," she began, "while we were setting up, I looked in the audience trying to find out where you were sitting. I thought you'd be sitting with my family. Of course, Richard talks so loud all the time that he was easy to locate. But you weren't there with him. At first I thought maybe you were going to be a little late. That was all right with me. I didn't have much to do in the first piece. By the beginning of the second piece, the houselights were off so I couldn't see into the audience, but I was certain you'd arrived by then. I wanted you to hear my solo. I had been working on this solo for months. I wanted to play it the best ever just for you."

She turned on the videotape. The sound of her trumpet was like an eagle gliding over a troubled sea. They watched two more pieces, and then she stopped the tape. "Now it was intermission," she said. "The houselights came up. I looked around hoping to find where you were. But you weren't around. I was the last one to leave the stage. I thought that maybe if you were there, you'd come down and tell me how well I'd done, but you didn't come. Richard did, though, and he gave me a big hug. He was the only one who knew how much I needed a hug."

Josh felt like he was being tortured.

"Not having you there when you said you'd come was

bad enough. But that wasn't all. During intermission a girl I know came up and said everyone was saying that you and I had been really going to it at the free-throw line in the gym. I asked her who told her, and she said Josh was telling everyone about it."

"I didn't tell anyone," Josh said.

"I guess I believe you now, but at that moment I felt like you'd chosen the one day when I needed support to dump on me. I felt so awful that someone I thought was a friend would treat me so badly."

"How many times do you want me to tell you I'm sorry?"

"As many times as it takes!" she shot back. "You really hurt me. I want you to know that. Once you do, then maybe we can move on from there. You think you can just say you're sorry and that'll take care of it? Well, it won't. I want us to keep going over this until we're both sick of it. I still don't understand why you didn't come to my concert after you said you'd be there."

"Kevin talked me into going to the party."

"Why does Kevin have so much power over you?"

"We've been friends for a long time."

"As long as you take advice about us from Kevin, you and I don't stand a chance."

"All right, look—from now on I'll eat lunch with you," he said.

"I have an earlier lunch period than you do."

"I can get mine changed."

"Nobody else can do it, so how come you can?" she asked.

"I just can, that's all."

"All right, do it then, but only if it's what you really want. What will Kevin say?"

"He'll say I'm crazy to let you call the shots," he said.

"You sure you want to do this then?"

"Yes, I am."

"All right then."

"Will you do something for me?" he asked.

"What?"

"I want you and Richard to come to church with me on Sunday. Will you do that?"

"I'll have to ask my mom and dad," she said.

"Let me ask them. They'll say yes."

"How do you know that?"

"Because they like me."

They drove over to Nicole's house and Josh did the asking.

"I don't suppose you'll take my word that it won't work out, will you?" Dave Stegman said.

"It's not that people mean to be unkind," Carol added. "It's just that the church isn't set up to deal with people like Richard."

"Nicole and I will be there to make sure things go okay."

"All right then, give it a try," Dave Stegman said. "But if I hear one word that Richard's been mistreated, that'll be the end of it."

"Everything will work out," Josh assured him.

"We've heard that all before," Carol said. "The way I see it, your church is mainly for people who don't have problems to get together and tell each other how wonderful they are. It didn't work before with Richard. It's not going to work now."

"This time it'll be different," Josh insisted.

"Well, I guess we'll see, won't we?" she said.

Josh got up at nine-thirty, an hour earlier than usual for a Sunday morning. He wanted to leave plenty of time to help Nicole get Richard ready for church. After getting dressed, he went into the kitchen. His father was at the kitchen table working on a lesson for the Sunday School class he taught.

Josh poured some cereal flakes in a bowl and sat down to eat breakfast.

"You're up early," his father said, at least partly teasing.

"Yeah, right. Please pass the milk."

Josh and his father didn't really talk much anymore. For one thing, they hardly ever saw one another. His father went to the TV station about three every weekday afternoon and stayed there until after the ten o'clock news. On Saturdays, he spent all morning doing the Willie the Rooster weather report, and on Saturday afternoons and evenings, Josh was usually gone.

But it was more than just that. When Josh needed permission to do something, he went to his mother. She would either say yes or that they needed to talk to his father. Josh would counter with, "I need to know today." Usually that was enough to get approval from her.

The issue about Josh having his own car had come up a year earlier. His grandfather on his mother's side had offered to buy him a car. His dad had said it was too expensive. His grandfather said, "We'll take care of it."

His dad had said it wasn't just the car—it was also the gas and oil and insurance. His grandfather said, "I'll take care of all that. He needs a car, even if it's just to get him to and from school."

Nearly out of patience, his father had said, "He's still my son, and I say no."

No more was said for a week, and then one day his mother told Josh his father had agreed to let him get a car.

A similar power play was now taking place, this time over college.

His father had saved money for college for his children, but most of it was gone by the time Kristen finished her first three years and turned twenty-one. What was left had gone into her mission fund.

Josh had begun his senior year with only seven hundred dollars in a savings account that was supposed to be used both for college and a mission. "What are you going to do about college and your mission?" his grandfather had asked him on the phone.

"I don't know. Go to State College, I guess. It's only about an hour from here."

"Who's ever heard of State College? A young man like you should be going to Harvard. Let me see what I can do, okay? Just send me a transcript of your grades, and I'll take care of the rest."

It turned out Josh's grades weren't good enough to get him into Harvard but his grandfather eventually managed to get him accepted at a private university in Boston. Josh needed to make up his mind what he was going to do. The university required a letter of acceptance, and the deadline was coming up soon.

And so, on that Sunday morning, many barriers separated Josh and his dad.

"Have you decided if you're going to Boston or not?" his dad asked.

"Not yet."

"I'm not sure you'll get that much better of an education there than you would if you lived at home and went to State."

"It won't cost you anything," Josh pointed out.

"You're wrong," his dad said. "What your grandfather is doing has already cost me a great deal."

Josh glanced up at his father and saw the hurt expression on his face. Josh was so embarrassed that he got up to make some toast. When he sat down again a few minutes later, everything was back to normal.

"Dad, have you heard anything from New York about them using you on Saturday mornings?" he asked.

"No, not yet."

"They'll want you, Dad, so don't worry, okay?"

"Sure they will. Thanks."

"Oh, I'm bringing Nicole and Richard to church today. We'll probably sit in the back."

"Do you need any help with him?" his father asked.

"I don't think so. Thanks for asking though."

When Nicole let him in, she was still in the sweats she used as pajamas. "I just woke up about ten minutes ago," she explained. "I can't seem to get Richard going."

"I came early to help out."

"Good. Will you ride herd on him while he gets dressed and make sure he eats breakfast while I get ready?"

"Sure, no problem. Where is he?"

"He's in his room."

On his way to Richard's room, Josh passed Nicole's room. He stopped and looked in. Her bed was unmade and there were clothes scattered on the floor. There was a music stand in the middle of the floor. The article about him from the sports page of the newspaper was tacked to her already cluttered bulletin board.

"Josh, that isn't fair," Nicole said from the bottom of the stairs.

His face turned red.

"I'm going to clean up after church," she said. "Now c'mon, please help get Richard ready."

He found Richard in his room watching cartoons on TV. He still had his pajamas on.

"Richard, do you want to come with Nicole and me?" he asked as he entered the room.

"Sure I do. What are we going to do?"

"We're going to church."

"I want to go to church," Richard said.

"Okay, but first you have to get dressed."

"Can I wear my Special Olympics medals to church?" Richard asked.

"Probably not."

"I'm a winner, Josh. Everyone in Special Olympics is a winner. Do you want to see my medals again?"

"Not now, we're kind of in a hurry. Maybe after church though. We need to turn the TV off so we can concentrate on getting dressed."

"But this is my favorite show," Richard protested.

"If you don't get dressed, you can't come to church with us."

"But this is my favorite show."

"Show me what clothes you want to wear to church. Pick out your best clothes, okay?"

"Okay." Richard went to the closet and showed Josh his best shirt and best pair of pants. "Why are we going to church?"

"To show Heavenly Father we love Him."

"Will He know that I'm at church?" Richard asked.

"Yes, He will," Josh said.

"How will He know?"

"He'll look down and see you there."

"He'll see me there?"

"Yes, He will, and that'll make Him happy."

Richard, by now in his underwear, grabbed his medals from off the wall. "I want to show Him my medals for Special Olympics."

Josh handed Richard the pair of pants they'd picked out. "Here, put these on. Heavenly Father has seen your medals."

"He has? When did He see them?"

"He looked down from heaven and saw you when you won them," Josh said.

"He saw me then too?"

"Yes, He can see us all the time."

"Can He see me now?" Richard asked.

"Yes, He can."

"If He can see us all the time, why do we have to go to church to tell Him we love Him? Why don't we just tell Him now, and then I won't have to miss my favorite TV show?"

"He wants us to go to church," Josh explained patiently.

"Why does He want us to go to church?"

Josh had to think about it. "Well, because . . . because He doesn't just want us to love Him—He wants us to love each other. And that's why we go to church, so we can learn to love each other."

"I love everybody in the whole world."

"I know you do, Richard. You're really good at that, better than anyone else. Can you zip up by yourself?"

Richard was annoyed by the question. "Yes."

"Good. Now the shirt."

"If I'm better at loving people than anybody, why do I have to go to church?"

"That's a good question. I think it's so people at church can learn to love you."

"Why do people need to learn to love me?" Richard said.

"Because Heavenly Father wants them to."

"Why?"

"Because they need to learn to love everyone, just like you do all the time already, if they want to go to heaven and live with Him someday. Because He's like you, Richard—He loves everyone. Whoa, stop, I think you're buttoning that wrong. First match up the bottom button with the bottom hole. Yeah, like that."

"I can get dressed by myself."

"I know you can. I'm just here to help."

"You love me, don't you?" Richard asked.

"Yes, I do." Josh looked in the closet to see if Richard had any dress shoes. He didn't see any. In fact, he couldn't see any shoes in the room. "Richard, where are your shoes?"

"I don't know."

"Do you think they're up here or downstairs?"

"I think downstairs."

"Okay, let's go down and see if we can find them. What do you want for breakfast?"

Even in socks Richard thundered down the stairs. "Pancakes. I love pancakes."

"I don't think we have time for pancakes. How about cereal?"

"Okay, but I can't have sugar in my cereal or I'll get sick," Richard said.

"Okay, no sugar."

"Also I can't have milk in my cereal because I'm allergic to milk."

"What do you have in your cereal?"

"Orange juice," Richard said.

Josh opened one cupboard after another until he found where they kept the cereal.

"It's good with orange juice. You want to try some?"

"If you say it's good, then I'll try it, because you're my friend," Josh said.

He opened the refrigerator and poured a little orange juice onto the bowl of cereal.

"A little more orange juice," Richard said.

"Okay. How's that?"

"Just the way I like it."

Josh tried a little cereal with orange juice. It wasn't that bad.

On their way to church, Richard said, "I can't wait for Heavenly Father to see me in church. He's going to be so happy."

They arrived at the church during the opening song. They sat in the overflow area of the chapel—Josh in the middle, with Nicole on his left and Richard on his right.

When they arrived, there were very few people in the back, but as the meeting progressed, the area filled up. Three boys who were about Richard's age came in late and began whispering and talking. It really annoyed Josh. When he turned around and glared, the boys stopped momentarily, but they started up again a short time later.

Richard sensed Josh's frustration. He turned around and, in a voice that could be heard throughout the chapel, said, "Heavenly Father can see you, so you'd better be quiet."

The boys broke out in partially hidden snickers. "Who's the retard?" one asked.

"Who cares? What I want to know is who's the babe?"

Josh got up and walked over to where the boys were sitting. "Either be quiet or go someplace else," he whispered loudly. Because he was six feet four and weighed one hundred and eighty pounds, the boys moved to another area of the back section.

During the first talk of the meeting, Richard said to Josh, "I want to go get a drink."

"I'll go with you," Josh replied.

In the hallway, Richard asked, "You're mad at those boys, aren't you?"

"Yes."

"Because they called me a retard?"

"Yes."

"That doesn't bother me."

At the end of sacrament meeting, after the Sunday School opening prayer and practice song, Josh remained seated in the overflow area and watched people file out. The Sunday School president came over, and Josh introduced Richard and Nicole. When the president offered to help them find their classes, Josh—knowing that Richard and the boys who had made fun of him would be in the same class—said he wasn't sure they were staying. His parents came up and said hello, but then they had to go because they both had classes to teach.

Several of the people who had sat in the back of the chapel had left the building as soon as sacrament meeting was over. For the first time Josh realized that it was possible to go to church and leave without saying hello or shaking anyone's hand.

Paul and Marilee Baxter stopped to greet him. "Josh, I see you have visitors today," Marilee said. "We'd like to meet them."

Josh stood up and introduced Nicole and Richard. "They're friends of mine," he explained.

"Hello, I'm Marilee Baxter and this is my husband, Paul," she said, reaching out to shake Richard's hand. "We've known Josh for a long time. He's our kids' hero."

"Yeah, what a guy," Paul Baxter said with a wry-looking grin. "He can eat more cookies than anyone else I've ever met. He eats us out of cookies once a month. How do you two know Josh?"

"From the state tournament," Josh said.

"Is she the one you were telling us about?"

"Yes."

"What exactly did he tell you?" Nicole asked.

"That you were the reason he did so well in the championship game," Marilee said.

"Wait a minute, I never said that."

"I know, but you should have," Marilee said. "You didn't tell us Nicole was such a beauty."

"Yes, how could you leave that out, Josh?" Nicole teased.

Paul turned to Richard and said, "Richard, what can you tell us about yourself?"

"I'm a winner."

"What a wonderful thing to be a winner," Paul said.

"We're so glad you came today, Richard. We hope you'll come back every week," Marilee added.

Josh decided that someday he wanted a wife who treated other people the way Marilee Baxter did.

"Paul, can I talk to you?" Josh asked. They moved a few feet away. "I don't know what to do about Sunday School class . . . you know, for Richard."

"You don't think it would work in his own age group?"

"No. Three boys who'd be in his class were making fun of him during sacrament meeting."

Paul nodded. "We can work it out, Josh. How about if Marilee and I have a special class for Richard? We'll need you and Nicole there with us though."

"Thank you," Josh said.

They met in the Baxters' van outside in the parking lot. It was a class Josh would never forget because of the comforting feeling he experienced. At times he almost could imagine that Heavenly Father really was looking down on them.

7

"Haven't seen you around much lately," Kevin said in the locker room after track practice on Monday.

"I have early lunch now."

"Right. You and the band chick, right?"

"She's not a chick. She's a girl, and her name's Nicole."

Kevin laughed. "Man, she's really got you nailed to the floor, doesn't she?"

"Yeah, right, and it's really awful. You know what I miss most? Those times when all of us used to pile in a car and drive around town and see who could belch the loudest. Gosh, those were the good old days."

"Hey, we still do that."

"I know you do. That's what's scary about you guys."

"You know what's scary about you?" Kevin asked.

"What?"

"You used to be a fighter but now you're all soft and warm and cuddly, like a big old Teddy Bear. Don't let her take over your life. You've got to show her who's boss."

"I'm learning a lot from her."

Kevin grinned. "She's really putting out for you then, huh?"

"Why don't you get your mind out of the gutter?" Josh burst out. "I can't even talk to you anymore."

On Saturday, after Josh and Nicole had spent the morning helping her father put in a new shower stall, they ended up in her driveway shooting baskets. At first Richard joined them; then he left to go shopping with his mother.

"The junior prom is coming up," Nicole said. She was shooting free throws. Josh retrieved the ball and passed it back.

"Yeah, so?"

"Are you going?" she asked.

"Haven't thought about it."

"What would you think about going with me?" she asked.

"I'd like that, except it's kind of expensive."

"We wouldn't have to spend that much," she said. "My mom and I could make the dress. I'll chip in some money to help you pay for renting a tux. We wouldn't have to eat out. We could eat here. C'mon, Josh, it won't kill you. Take me to the prom."

"You're not supposed to ask me. I'm supposed to ask you."

"Ask me then."

"I'll tell you what. We'll play a little one-on-one. If I lose, I'll take you to the prom."

"Yeah, sure, like that's really fair," she said.

"Even it out then. What do you want? For me to only be able to shoot left-handed? Pick anything and I'll go along with it."

"Anything? Okay, I want you blindfolded," she said.

"Like that's really fair."

"Hey, you're the one who said pick anything."

Nicole got a ski mask from her room and brought it back for Josh to put on. Then she led him to the center of the court. He had put the ski mask on backwards and could see a little, though she didn't know it.

"Can you see anything?" she asked.

"Not a thing," he lied.

"Good. Then you won't mind if I put a scarf over the mask."

By the time she finished, Josh really couldn't see anything. "I can't breathe," he complained.

"You faker. The scarf is just over your eyes. You ready?"

"I'll probably still beat you, 'cause I'll know where you're at by just listening to you dribble the ball."

He heard the sound of the ball hitting the rim.

"Okay, that's two points for me," she said.

"Wait a minute. You can't just walk up to the basket and shoot. I never heard you dribble. That means you traveled."

"Did you see me travel?" she asked.

"No, but I didn't hear the ball bounce."

"Easy to explain. I shot from midcourt. Okay, two to zero, my favor. Now it's your turn to take the ball in."

"Wait a minute. I need to pace out where the basket is." He started to walk toward what he thought was the direction of the basket. She grabbed the ball and went in for another layup.

"Four to zero, my favor," she said.

"I had time-out."

"You didn't say time-out."

"I said, 'Wait a minute.' "

"Sorry. The rule is you have to say time-out."

Ten minutes later it was over. "Thanks for the game, Josh," she said, as she untied the scarf. "Let's do this again sometime. Maybe after the prom, okay?"

When Josh got home that night, his mother told him that the national network people had called his father and told him they had decided not to go with "Willie the Rooster and His Wacky Weather." "Your father is pretty disappointed," she said.

Josh was sorting through the newspaper, looking for the sports section. "I suppose," he said, without feeling. He found it and started to read the headlines.

His mother knocked the paper out of his hand. "Josh Dutton, sometimes I could just shake you!"

"What'd I do?"

"Don't you even care what happens to your father?"

"Sorry. It's just that it's kind of hard to feel sorry for Dad when he's in his rooster costume."

"You watch what you're saying, young man. Do you know why he wanted this so much? It was so he'd be able to bring in some extra money to help you with college and your mission."

"It's taken care of."

"Yes, and that's all you care about, isn't it?"

"What are you saying?" he complained.

"I'm saying you should be learning all you can from your father, instead of ignoring him the way you do."

"What else can I do but ignore him? He's never home."

"You could arrange to spend some time with him if you wanted to. Do you know what I'm afraid of? That you're going to go away to college back East and my father is going to turn you into a snob like the men my sisters married. Okay, so we don't have as much money as they do, but money isn't everything. We're happy, we have enough to get by, and your father is doing what he most loves to do. Just don't write him off, Josh. There's a lot he could teach you if you'd let him."

On the night of the prom, Josh showed up at Nicole's home at six. Richard opened the door, took one look at him in his black tux, and started laughing. "You look like a penguin, just like my dad said you would," he said.

"Gosh, Richard, talk about hurting a guy's feelings." Josh smiled to show he wasn't serious.

"I was just kidding. You should see Nicole. She looks pretty! My mom says you're a lucky guy, but I think Nicole's the lucky one because you're the best basketball player in the state."

"Maybe so, but not blindfolded," Josh said.

"You look good and you smell good. Nicole does too. You want to come in and have Ritz crackers with stuff on 'em? Also we have bread sticks, except I've eaten most of 'em. Don't tell on me though, okay?"

"I won't. It really looks nice in here," Josh said.

"We worked on it all day. I helped too. You want to sit down? I vacuumed the cat hairs, so sit anywhere you want."

"Gosh, Richard, it's so clean I don't even know where to begin to sit."

"Sit here in front of the TV. Except you can't watch TV. This is a special night, and my mom says we can't watch TV on a special night."

Josh sat down.

Richard was too excited to sit down. He paced the room as he talked. "Nicole's been getting ready since this morning," he said. "My mom and Nicole worked on the dress all night and even this morning. What did you do to get ready?"

"I took a shower."

"Boys have it easy, don't they?"

"You're right, Richard."

Carol Stegman came into the room. "Hi, Josh," she greeted him. "Has Richard been taking good care of you?"

"Oh yes. Richard and I always have a great time together."

"You look very handsome tonight," she said.

"Thanks. Richard told me that you went to a lot of trouble making Nicole's prom dress."

"Things like that always take longer than you think.

After we finished last night, I had Nicole put it on. It wasn't as modest as I thought it should be, so this morning we added some lace."

"You didn't need to go to so much trouble . . . that is . . . I mean . . . "

"Don't worry about it," she said.

Nicole came down the stairs to the living room. Josh was astonished. He felt he didn't have the right to even be in the same room with her, much less be her date for a prom. "Oh, my gosh," he said. "You look great."

"Thanks. So do you."

"All Josh did was take a shower," Richard said.

Josh glanced at the lace bodice and then turned to Nicole's mom and said, "You did a good job. I can't see anything." He realized this was not going well.

Nicole took mercy and changed the subject. "Well, Josh, are you ready to take me to a fine restaurant where we will dine in luxury?"

"Yes, of course. Nothing but the best for you, even if you do cheat at one-on-one basketball."

Nicole smiled. "Mother, Josh and I are now going to a very fine restaurant."

"Have a nice time. Oh, wait. Before you go, we need to take pictures."

"Can I be in the picture?" Richard asked.

"We'll take one with you in the picture, but the rest will be just Josh and Nicole."

"Can I be in the first picture?" Richard asked.

"Yes, but first wash your hands. I don't want you making a mess on Nicole's dress."

When Richard returned from washing his hands, they were ready to have their picture taken. Nicole stood in the middle with Richard and Josh on either side. After the pictures were taken, Josh and Nicole drove away in his car. They drove around the neighborhood for a few minutes, then returned to her house. As they pulled up, they saw Richard holding a hand-painted sign that read "Famous Restaurant."

They entered the house again. Richard, dressed in a white shirt and blue slacks, greeted them and said, "Hello, I'm Richard. Do you want to eat here?"

"Yes, we do."

"You have to follow me."

They would be the first ones to eat in the new dining room Dave Stegman had just finished. Richard led them to the center of the room, where a card table, draped with a white linen tablecloth, had been set up. "Want something to drink?" he asked. "We have grape juice with Seven-Up in it," he told them formally, but then, breaking character and almost whispering, he added, "It's really good. I snuck a taste. Don't tell anyone. Here's a menu."

The hand-lettered menu read:

1. Roast Beef with baked potato, corn, dinner rolls, salad, and pie à la mode.

2. Crab. We're out of crab. Go for the roast beef.

3 Chicken. We're out of chicken too. Pick the roast beef.

"Richard, did you drink the grape juice?" they heard Carol Stegman ask from the kitchen.

"No."

"You'd better not have because it had sugar in it. It's just for Nicole and Josh, so don't have any."

"He already did," Nicole called out, somewhat breaking the mood.

"Richard, you get in here. We need to talk."

They could hear the rumble in the other room as Carol laid the law down to Richard. A few minutes later, he came out with their beverages. "We have a waiter too. Want to see him?"

He returned to the kitchen, and a short time later Dave

Stegman came out with a dish towel over his arm. He was wearing a white dress shirt and slacks, and sporting a wig of curly black hair and a very silly horsehair mustache. Speaking in a false French accent, he said, "Good evening. My name is Chief Vaiter Maurice, and I vill be your vaiter zis evening."

Nicole burst out laughing.

"Pardonnnn," he said. "Is something amiss, miss?"

"Sorry," she said, trying to force herself to be serious.

"Are ze gentleman and ze lady ready to order?"

"Yes, we will have the roast beef," Josh said.

"Excellent choice. Vat vould you like on your salad?"

"Vat . . . er, what do you have?"

"Ve have French dressing."

"We'll have that."

"Excellent choice." Dave clapped his hands and called out. "Ze number one with ze French dressing."

By this time Nicole was giggling uncontrollably.

"Perhaps ze lady finds something amusing about my attire?"

"Which tire? The one you have around your middle?" she teased.

"I have never been so insulted in my life." He turned on his heel and left the room.

The meal was excellent, the service good, although every time her father came out, Nicole started giggling. After dessert, she and Josh went into the kitchen to thank the staff. She kissed the cook on the cheek and hugged the waiter and got hugged by the maitre d'.

"Can I come and see you dance?" Richard asked.

"No, Richard, this isn't for you," Nicole said.

"Just for a while."

"No."

"Please."

"It's up to Josh," she said.

"Josh will let me. Won't you, Josh?"

"You can come if your mom or dad wants to bring you."

"It will just be for a minute," Nicole's father said.

Josh parked outside the school and reached into one of his tuxedo pants pockets. "I got you something," he said, handing her a small box. "Go ahead, open it."

She undid the wrapping and opened the box. Inside was a jade necklace. "It's beautiful," she whispered.

"It's jade. It's the same color as your eyes."

"This is the nicest gift I've ever received. Thank you. I absolutely love it."

"It was my mom's idea to get you something, but I picked it out."

He helped fasten the clasp of the necklace, and then they walked arm in arm into the gym, where the dance was being held. The theme of the dance was "Magical Kingdom." Crepe paper was taped to the walls and draped from the ceiling to make it seem not so much like a gymnasium.

Kevin was there with Kim, one of Nicole's roommates at the state tournament. As soon as he saw Josh and Nicole, he came over. Josh could smell alcohol on his breath. "This must seem like old times for you two. Oh, the free-throw line is over there," he said, in a snide tone.

"Knock it off," Josh said.

"Sorry. Oh, Josh, I have to talk to you alone, it's kind of important."

They excused themselves and walked over to the sidelines, where Kevin put his hand on Josh's shoulder and spoke confidentially. "A couple of us have rented a motel room for tonight. We're renting out time slots. The next opening is between two and three in the morning. It's only ten dollars, but you've got to make the bed as best as you can for the ones coming after. I need the money now though."

"This is the first time you've been out with Kim, isn't it?"

"What's that got to do with anything? She knows all about my plans."

"Let me talk to her."

"You stay away from her," Kevin warned. "What about you and the band chick? You want me to put you down for some time?"

"You're hopeless, you know that?"

"Oh? Is that a fact? Well, at least I don't abandon my friends."

Josh returned to Nicole. She took one look at him and said, "Let's go take a walk, okay?"

They made their way down the empty halls of the school.

"All right, tell me what he said," she said, turning to him.

He told her all about Kevin's plan.

"I'm not surprised," she commented. "It sounds like him. So why is it making you so mad?"

"Kevin and I have been best friends ever since I moved here. He talked me into trying out for the ninth grade basketball team. So why is he acting like such a jerk all of a sudden?"

"I don't know. I'm just glad you're not around him much anymore."

They could hear the music in the distance. She put her head on his chest and they swayed to the rhythm. With her high heels, she was tall enough for them to dance cheek to cheek. She exuded a cloud of aromas and softness and beauty. It felt as if they were floating in air.

"One time my dad told me that my mom was his best friend," Josh said. "I can see how that happens. I guess you're my best friend now."

"Good for me."

They danced in the hallway for a couple of songs and then started back. As they approached the gym, Josh saw Kevin and Kim slipping out. He looked at his watch and figured that Kevin and Kim had an hour before it was someone else's turn. He knew that on Monday the guys he used to eat lunch with, who used to talk about exciting plays of a football game, would each tell about their hour in the motel. He was glad he wouldn't be there to listen to them.

At nine-thirty Richard and his father showed up at the dance. Josh could hear Richard the minute he walked in the gym. Josh and Nicole were dancing. When the song ended, Richard walked over to them at the edge of the dance floor. He looked around in awe and amazement at the way the gym was decorated. "Wow! This is like *Beauty and the Beast!*" he exclaimed, his voice carrying through the whole gym.

"Who's the Beauty?" Nicole asked.

"You are," Richard said.

"Thank you, Richard. That's very sweet." Then, with a smile, she added, "So, let's see. If I'm the Beauty, then I wonder who the Beast is?"

"Josh is the Beast."

"Hey, wait a minute, Richard. You think I'm a beast?" Josh asked.

"No, but you love Nicole, and she's the Beauty, so you have to be the Beast."

"Yes, that's the way it has to be," Nicole said, touching Josh on the tip of his nose. "So there, you big beast."

Dave Stegman, who had stopped to talk to one of the parents who was chaperoning the dance, came over to them. He had put on a sport coat so he would look a little more acceptable at the dance. "Richard, we need to go now," he said.

Richard looked up at the crepe-paper-draped ceiling. "This is like a paper castle," he said, still in awe.

Dave put his hand on his son's arm. "Yes, it is. I'm glad you got to see it. Let's go. Say good-bye to Nicole and Josh."

"Josh, don't you think this is like *Beauty and the Beast?"*

"You mean the part where they were dancing?" Josh asked Richard.

"Yes, it's just like *Beauty and the Beast."*

"It is, Richard, it really is," Nicole agreed. "I can see exactly what you mean."

Richard gave them each a big hug and then left with his father.

As the evening wore on, more and more people left early. Some, like Kevin and his friends, ended up in motel rooms, some in cars in the parking lot drinking, most at small parties in homes and restaurants. Josh and Nicole didn't care what anyone else did because they had each other. Their world had shrunk to one corner of a gym floor.

A photographer from a local studio was taking pictures. "Let's get our picture taken," Josh said.

"We can't."

"Why can't we?"

"We didn't budget for it."

"My dad gave me some money. Besides, I want to always remember how beautiful you are tonight."

"Wait a minute—are you the same guy who drags me out into the cold to shoot baskets?" she asked.

"Yeah, that's me."

"Amazing what a tux will do, isn't it? Are we going to clown around or be serious for the picture?" she asked.

"Let's see if we can make people believe we're in love," he said.

"Yes, let's do that," she whispered softly.

The last half hour featured all slow songs. They closed their eyes and rocked slowly to the rhythm. When the last dance was over, they stayed wrapped up in each other's arms. "I guess it's over," she said.

"I guess so."

"Thanks, Josh. I'll always remember this night."

"Me too."

Someone turned on the lights, and the room became a gym with crepe paper that needed to be thrown away.

"I went to the prom with Josh Dutton!" Nicole called out to the whole world. "We had a wonderful time and nobody can take that away from us!" She threw her arms around him and they kissed. The kiss began in a silent room but ended with the sounds of people talking loudly and tearing things down.

"Unless you signed us up for the cleanup committee," Josh whispered in her ear, "we need to get out of here."

"I know. It's just that I don't want this night to end. It's like being at the end of your life and you're about to die. And you think about all the things you didn't do while you were alive, and all you want is just a little more time. That's what this is like. This is my one and only prom and I don't want it to end."

They drove to Josh's house, where his parents had prepared some snacks for them. After they ate Josh changed into jeans and a sweatshirt, and they left to go to Nicole's so she could change. A parent committee from the high school had reserved a bowling alley and game room for students to go to after the prom. Josh had challenged Nicole to a bowling marathon.

As soon as they pulled into her driveway, she said, "Something's wrong."

"How do you know?"

"Richard's light is on."

Even as they opened the door to go inside, they could hear Richard groaning.

"He's having a seizure," she said.

They ran up the stairs to Richard's room. He was thrashing around on his bed. Dave and Carol Stegman were kneeling over him, trying to prevent him from hurting himself.

"Josh is here," Nicole said to Richard between seizures.

"I had sugar," Richard moaned.

"I'm sorry you're having a rough time," Josh said.

"Don't go, okay?"

"Okay."

Nicole brought in a chair from her room for Josh and then went to change clothes. When she returned a few minutes later, she went up behind Josh in his chair and leaned over and whispered in his ear, "You don't have to stick around. I know you're tired. Why don't you go home and get some sleep?"

"Richard asked me to stay, so I will."

"Mom," Nicole said, "Josh and I can watch him for a while if you and Dad want to get some sleep."

"No, this is your prom night."

"We don't mind," Josh said.

"Besides," Nicole said, "Richard is probably going to sleep anyway, but if anything happens, we'll let you know."

Her parents suggested that Josh call his folks and let them know where he was. His father answered. Josh explained what had happened and said that he wanted to stay for the night with Richard. Because of that, he might not make it to church the next day. His father agreed and thanked him for calling.

Nicole curled up in an old recliner, draped a blanket

over herself, and went to sleep. Josh slept on the floor in Richard's sleeping bag.

The next thing Josh remembered, it was morning and Richard was kneeling down near where he was sleeping.

"Josh," Richard said.

"What?"

"I'm okay now."

Josh sat up. "That's really good. I was worried about you."

"This was like an overnight, wasn't it?"

"Yes, I guess it was."

"Not a very good overnight though."

"No, not very good."

"Nicole's a sleepy head."

"I know. She's tired. We'd better not wake her up."

"You love her, don't you?" Richard asked.

"Yes."

"You should marry her someday and then I'd be your uncle."

"Actually, I think you'd be my brother-in-law," Josh explained.

Richard looked disappointed. "I'd rather be your uncle."

"Well, you'd be an uncle to our kids. How would that be?"

"Good. I think you should get married right away."

"I have to go on a mission first," Josh said.

"I want to go on a mission too."

"Where do you want to go on your mission?"

Richard thought about it for a while. "Disneyland."

"I don't think they have missionaries at Disneyland."

"They should. I would go up to people while they were waiting and tell them about our church. And when it was their turn to ride, they'd be ready to be baptized."

"That's a great idea, Richard."

"I love you, Josh. You're my best friend."

"I am?"

"Yes, the very best."

"My very best friend is Nicole," Josh said, "but you're my next best friend."

As they talked, Richard became tired. Finally he fell asleep. Josh lay down and slept too. He woke up again at one-thirty in the afternoon. Too late for church. It was the first time he had missed church in a long time. He got up and went downstairs. Carol Stegman was reading the newspaper at the kitchen table. She asked him what he wanted to eat. He told her he'd wait for Nicole to get up and then eat with her. She said she'd saved a sticky bun for him from the day before.

"Thank you for staying with Richard last night," she said, as she set a plate with a bun and a glass of milk in front of him. "You've been so good to him. He really looks up to you."

"Richard and I are buddies. How often does he get sick like this?"

"Two or three times a month."

"Must be hard on him—" he thought for a moment about it "—and on you too."

"Yes, at times it's very hard."

"What's been the hardest thing you've had to go through?"

She paused before answering. "Facing the truth. At first I tried to prove everyone wrong. I remember trying to teach him our phone number by turning it into a song. I thought that if I just worked with him, everything would be all right." She went to the refrigerator and refilled Josh's milk glass.

"What happened?" he asked.

"Eventually I realized they were right and I was wrong."

"That must have been hard on you," he commented.

"It was one of the low points of my life. I still can't read Christmas letters where parents brag about their children."

"How is it for you now?" he asked.

"I've become a fighter in my old age. I make sure Richard gets everything he's entitled to. You wouldn't believe how confusing it all was at first—school administrators tossing out phrases that I'd never heard about. And yet these people have the power to say whether Richard is eligible or not for some federal programs. Now I know as much as they do. I'm sure they dread seeing me walk into their offices. But I don't care what they think. I only care about my son."

"You're a lot tougher than you look, aren't you?"

She smiled. "I'm as tough as nails, Josh. If anyone crosses Richard or Nicole, they'll have to answer to me."

"Thanks for the warning."

"I'm not worried about you and Nicole, not one bit. We think of you as just part of the family." She paused. "Of course that has a downside too. It means you're fair game now."

"Fair game for what?"

She hid a smile. "Oh, nothing."

The "oh, nothing" happened a week later, when Josh was invited for supper at Nicole's house.

"We thought we'd eat in the living room tonight," Carol Stegman said. "That way we can watch a movie while we're eating."

Nicole took Josh aside and said, "Just one warning. We had the carpet cleaned yesterday, so try and not spill anything, okay?"

"Sure, no problem." To be truthful, Josh didn't think the carpet looked all that good for having just been cleaned.

Dave Stegman cut a thick piece of roast beef for Josh and plopped it on a flimsy paper plate, then added a huge portion of mashed potatoes and gravy. He also gave him a big glass of grape juice. The portions he gave to Nicole were much smaller. Josh also noticed that her paper plate seemed sturdier.

Nicole accompanied him to the living room. "There're TV trays for us to eat on," she said. "You sit there and I'll be here."

The TV tray in front of the couch where she asked him to sit looked as if it were about to fall apart. Soon everyone but Josh was eating. As he started to cut a piece of the roast beef, the tray leaned precariously. He looked around. Nobody else seemed to be having any trouble. He decided to hold the plate in his hand because he didn't trust the TV tray, but the problem then was that he couldn't cut his meat. He sat staring at his plate.

"Aren't you hungry, Josh?" Dave asked.

"Yeah, sure. Just slow getting started."

He tried to rest the plate on his knees and cut the meat, but as he did so, the plate buckled and a little gravy ran out onto the floor. "Oh, gosh. I'm really sorry."

"Josh," Nicole said quietly as she helped him clean up, "try to be a little more careful from now on, okay?"

"This plate is too flimsy."

"Really? Nobody else seems to be having any trouble."

He gave up on the meat and concentrated on the potatoes and green beans. "Josh, could you get me some pepper in the kitchen?" Nicole asked.

As he got up he didn't even touch the TV tray, but one step later he heard Nicole cry out. He turned around to see his TV tray on its side. His plate and the glass of grape juice had spilled onto the carpet.

Josh felt awful. "I'll clean it up," he said.

Nicole couldn't stand to see Josh feeling bad for very long. She came to his side, put her hand on his forearm, and, in her sweetest voice, said, "I have a tiny little confession to make."

"What?"

"We're getting new carpet tomorrow."

"You are?"

"Yes, and since they're going to rip out the old carpet anyway, I thought it wouldn't matter, you know, if it had a few stains on it. So . . . "

It was beginning to sink in. "You set me up?"

"Yes. It worked pretty good too, didn't it?"

Josh threw his hands into the air and roared with laughter. "Oh, my gosh! I can't believe it! You guys really got me, didn't you?"

"We played a big joke on you, didn't we, Josh?" Richard teased.

"The best joke anybody's ever done on me, Richard, and that's a fact."

"I just want you to know this wasn't my idea," Carol protested.

"Mine either," Dave confessed, "at least not at first, but then, I don't know, after a while I really got into it."

After getting a new plate of food for Josh, they ate the rest of the meal at the dining room table. Nicole tried to make up for the joke by anticipating his every need. She made sure he had plenty to eat and filled his juice and water glasses several times during the meal.

After supper he and Nicole and Richard went outside to shoot baskets. "I'll get you for this, Nicole, if it's the last thing I do," he said, as he began to dribble the ball.

"Yeah, sure, just like you always do."

8

The next Friday there was a regional track meet in town. Josh was scheduled to run the 800-meter race in the late afternoon. Just before his race Brandy Wilson showed up with the Special Olympics team to cheer him on. They came down to the first row of the stands. Josh was on the football field doing stretching exercises when they arrived. Suddenly he heard familiar voices.

"There he is!"

"Where?"

"Right there."

"I don't see him."

"He's pulling on his leg to warm up."

"I see him. Hi, Josh! Look, he waved at me."

"Hi, Josh!"

"Hi, Josh!"

"Hi, Josh!"

"Hi, Josh!"

"Hi, Josh!"

"Hi, Josh!"

"Everyone sit down and be quiet!" Brandy's voice rang out. "We have to let Josh warm up."

"Hi, Josh!"

"David, did you hear what I just said?" Brandy's voice shouted.

Josh got up and walked over to the fence. "Hi, you guys! Thanks for coming."

"We came to watch you run!"

"Wow, that's great! Thanks, guys."

Brandy called out, "David, quit pushing. There's room for everyone."

"I can't see."

"Can you come sit with us after your race?" Richard asked.

"I don't know. I'll ask my coach. If he says it's okay, then I will, okay?"

"Okay."

"Our cat had kittens," a girl called out to him.

"Last night?" Josh asked.

"No. A long time ago."

"Oh, that must have been interesting to watch."

"Everybody sit down!" Brandy shouted again. She yelled down to Josh. "Get out of here, Josh. You're making it hard for me to keep control of these guys. Oh, by the way, good luck."

"Thanks."

"Bye, Josh."

"Bye, Josh."

"Good luck, Josh."

"Bye, Josh."

"Bye, Josh."

"Bye, Josh."

He went to the middle of the football field to warm up. Kevin, who threw discus for their school, came up to him. "So, what's going on? You bring all your cousins to cheer for you?" he asked.

"Something like that."

"I'm serious. Who are they?"

"Special Olympics."

"Oh, right, that's what you use as your excuse for skipping practice once a week. The coach told us all about it. I got to tell you, it brought tears to all our eyes. You are just so full of goodness, aren't you, sweet cakes?"

"That's right."

"Too bad you're going to lose big time today."

"What makes you think that?"

"You've lost your competitive edge. You've become warm and fuzzy. That band chick has ruined you for good."

"Why is it when I spend time with a girl, it's bad, but when you do, it's okay."

"Because I don't let 'em get to me. I use 'em, then lose 'em. Like Kim. After the prom she was getting too possessive so I cut her loose. I'm serious about you losing in the 800-meter race today."

"I have the state record."

"Sure, last year. This is a whole new ball game, Josh. Hampton has a freshman named Sloan. They say he's somebody to watch out for."

"A freshman?" Josh scoffed. "Yeah, right, I'll bet he's a holy terror."

"If you weren't so wrapped up in the band chick and Special Olympics, you probably wouldn't have any trouble with him. But let's face it, you're a cream puff now."

Before the race, as each runner lined up behind the starting line, Josh looked over the competition. He had raced against all but two of the other runners before. Just like the ones he'd beaten before, he knew they'd be no competition. Then he stared at Sloan. The guy didn't appear to even know who Josh was. That bothered Josh.

Josh looked at the track and reviewed his strategy. They had to run twice around the track. The first lap, he would stay in the pack. The second lap, he would sprint, pull ahead of everyone else until he dashed all hopes of their ever catching him, and then coast to victory.

The race was about to begin. The sound from the crowd seemed to disappear. Time seemed to slow down.

The shot was fired and the race began. The runners stayed bunched up for only 100 meters and then Sloan, the freshman, shot out ahead of everyone else, sprinting. Josh knew Sloan was doing this because of his lack of experience. He was expending too much energy and he wouldn't have enough to keep him going. Then his lead would get smaller, and finally, halfway around the final lap, Josh would pour it on and pass him.

But Sloan's lead kept increasing. Josh became worried. *What if he keeps this up?* he thought. Sloan had forced Josh out of his plan, and Josh sped up, trying to catch him. *I'm not going to have anything left,* he told himself as he cut the distance between him and Sloan to half.

As the runners passed by the stands, Josh's coach yelled out his time. Josh was two seconds off his best time, and yet he felt as if he were running faster than he had ever run before. Sloan gave no sign of tiring out. Josh knew he had to dig deep to come up with the will, no matter how it hurt, to pour it on, to pull even with Sloan, and then, somehow, to sprint past him just before the finish line.

Maybe Kevin was right. Maybe I should have been more serious about this, he told himself. *Not now. Just run.* He willed himself to decrease the distance between him and Sloan. Sloan heard him coming and looked back.

Never look back, Josh muttered under his breath. He pulled up next to Sloan, who glanced at him, smiled, then put on a burst of speed. They were rounding the final curve before the finish line.

Sloan was still ahead of him.

Josh didn't have anything left.

I just let a freshman beat me, he thought.

Sloan breezed across the finish line. Josh was next. He slowed down and nearly collapsed. His lungs felt as if they were on fire. His coach ran up to him and put his arms around him. "You okay?"

Josh shook his head. "That guy's not human. He did everything wrong. Started too soon." He felt his knees getting weak.

"He'll get better."

"That's what worries me. What was my time?"

"Half a second from your best time last year. And this is only his first race. What's he going to be like by the time the state meet rolls around?"

The coach left, and Josh walked around trying to catch his breath. Sloan came over. He had a big smile on his face and didn't seem to be having any trouble breathing. "Good job," he said in a boyish voice.

"Yeah, you too. Do you know who I am?"

"They said you set a record last year at state," Sloan said.

"That's right."

"That was last year though, right?"

After he cooled down, Josh went up in the stands and sat with the Special Olympics team.

"You're a winner," Richard said.

Josh smiled and gave him a hug. Richard made everything seem better.

The next day in church, after the sacrament had been passed, the bishop announced that the Primary children would sing. He asked the children to come up to the stand. Before they could stop him, Richard was on his way to the front. Because Josh and Nicole were afraid going up to get him would cause too much commotion, they let him go. He ended up on the back row, surrounded by kids much shorter than he.

Nobody knew what to do, so they tried to ignore him and go ahead with the performance. Richard sang much louder than anyone else, but he didn't know all the words. For phrases he didn't know, he hummed. By the time the first song was over, it was clear the situation could not continue. Josh went up and got him.

"This is just for little kids," Josh said quietly. They walked back to their seats. They made it through the rest of the meeting with no other problem. When it was time to go to Sunday School class, the Sunday School president suggested that Josh and Nicole go with Richard to his class just to see if it would work out having him in with his own age group.

When they walked into the class, the instructor stopped talking. Josh made the introductions. "This is Richard," he said, "and this is his sister, Nicole. This is the class Richard should be in."

The back row was taken up by boys who didn't want to get involved in the lesson. There were two girls in the first row. Richard, Nicole, and Josh sat in the first row.

Josh put his head down, trying to appear inconspicuous. At first it was quiet, but soon he heard the boys behind him making fun of Richard.

The teacher, struggling to hold their attention, asked an easy question. "Who do we need to thank for even being alive?" he asked.

Richard raised his hand.

"Yes?"

"Heavenly Father."

"That's right, Heavenly Father."

One of the boys in back mimicked Richard's manner of speaking. That caused the others to laugh. When the teacher asked them to be quiet, one of them started to giggle, setting the others off. Josh got up and sat in the middle of the back row in an effort to keep them quiet.

The rest of the lesson went better, but it was a shallow victory because the boys did not forget.

The next Friday Josh had another track meet. He won his race convincingly, which helped his self-confidence, but Sloan was not there. The next day Josh read in the newspaper that Sloan, the day before, had easily won his race at another track meet, beating Josh's best time from last year. Josh realized that the only thing that would keep him from winning another state title would be Sloan.

Every Saturday morning the boys in the ward got together at the church to play basketball. It had begun as an Aaronic Priesthood activity that was chaperoned by one of the Aaronic Priesthood advisers, but over the course of time, with people moving from the ward and new ones moving in, there were times when no adult was present to make sure things didn't get out of hand.

Josh asked Nicole's mother if it would be all right if he took Richard to play basketball at church. She gave her permission. Nicole asked if she could come along for the ride.

By the time they got there, a game was already in progress. Josh went over and talked to one of the boys. "Richard and I want to play next game," he said. "We'll be on the same team, so when he plays, I play."

"Can he even play?"

"Yes, actually he's pretty good. How long will it be until you can put us in for a few minutes?"

"Fifteen more minutes."

"Great."

They sat down and watched for a few minutes. Then Nicole and Josh went out in the hall to get a drink and left Richard watching the game. They ended up outside on the steps talking.

A few minutes later a boy came out of the building. "You'd better come quick!" he advised them.

"What's wrong?"

It was too awful to say. "You'd better come quick."

They hurried inside. As they approached the gym, they could hear loud laughter. The boy who had gotten them said, "I didn't do it. I told them they shouldn't do it."

They entered the gym. There, standing in the center of a group of boys, was Richard in his underpants. "Where's your pants, retard?" one of the boys was taunting. "What if a girl comes in? What'll you do then?"

Suddenly the boys realized Josh had come back. They watched as he went over to Richard. "What happened, Richard?"

"They took my pants and hid them. They won't give them back."

Josh turned and glared at each of the boys in the circle. "Where are his pants?"

Nobody said a thing.

"Get me his pants!" he roared.

"I didn't do it," a boy called out, standing up, "but I know where they are."

"Go get them."

The boy ran down the hall.

"Who did this?" Josh demanded.

Silence.

He grabbed one of the boys who had made fun of Richard on Sunday and asked, "Was it you?"

"I didn't do anything."

"Who did?"

Nicole grabbed Josh's hand, which held the boy by his collar. "They all did it," she said. "You can't beat them all up, Josh. Just let it be."

Josh let go.

A boy returned with Richard's pants and gave them to him.

"Thank you," Josh said, just barely managing to stay in

control. "How could you do this? How could you be so cruel?"

As soon as Richard was dressed, they left the building and drove away. "Richard, what those boys did is wrong," Nicole said, "but I don't think we should tell Mom and Dad about it."

"Why not?" Richard asked.

"Because they might not let us go to church anymore if they find out."

"That would be bad."

"So will you promise not to tell them?" Nicole asked.

"Okay."

The secret lasted half an hour after they arrived at Nicole's house. Then Richard, dressed only in his underpants, came into the kitchen where his mother, Josh, and Nicole were talking.

"Richard, get your clothes on," his mother said.

"Look, I have a bruise," he said.

"How did you get it?"

"It was when the boys pushed me down."

"What boys?"

"The boys at church."

"Were you wrestling with them?"

"No, it was when they pulled my pants off."

She turned to Nicole and Josh and asked, "What's he talking about?"

"Some boys at the gym pantsed Richard," Josh said.

"And you two weren't going to tell me about it?" her mother said.

"We knew how upset it would make you."

"So you decided to cover it up?"

"Yes," Nicole said. "Do we have to tell Daddy about this?"

"Yes, we have to. We can't start hiding things from each other. Once you start that, there's no end to it."

Josh stayed at Nicole's until Dave Stegman came home. As soon as Dave entered the house, Josh explained what had happened.

"Now you can see why we quit going to church in the first place," Dave commented grimly. "They talk a good line, but when it comes to putting it in practice, nothing ever comes of it."

"It was my fault," Josh said. "I never should have left him there alone with those boys."

Dave turned to Nicole and asked, "How can you keep going to a church that treats your brother like that?"

"Daddy, you can't blame the church, because Josh belongs to the church too, and you know how much he's done for Richard."

"It's not going to get any better, you know," her mother said. "The church just isn't set up to deal with people with special needs. You'll find that out. You're just going to keep getting disappointed. I think you should quit now before you get your feelings even more hurt than they are now. My son gets better treatment any other place he goes than he gets at church."

"It's just that they don't know him like I do," Josh said.

"They've had their chance to get to know him and look what they've done with it," Dave said. "I'd be a fool if I ever let him go back there again."

Later that day, Josh and Nicole were alone together in the driveway shooting baskets. "My folks know you feel bad about it, Josh," she said. "And don't worry about Richard. He's not going to have any bad feelings about it. He never does."

Josh nodded. "I suppose."

"Talk to me, Josh."

"Why don't people at church care about Richard?" Josh asked.

"You care about him."

"That's not enough."

"It's better than nothing."

He stopped dribbling the ball. She came over to him, and they wrapped their arms around each other and hugged. It was something they had learned from Richard.

9

The next day, Sunday, Ellis Dutton woke Josh up at nine-thirty. "Your mother and I need to go to church early," he explained, "so you're on your own as far as getting up and getting ready for church."

"Why do you have to go so early?" Josh asked.

"The stake president wants to talk to us."

"What for?"

"He didn't say."

An hour later, when his parents returned, Josh was still in bed. They knocked on the door and came in.

"Josh, are you awake? We need to talk to you," his mother said, coming over to his bed.

Josh sat up. "What is it?"

"They're calling a new bishopric today," she explained. "Your father has been asked to serve as first counselor."

"What did you tell them?"

"I told him what my schedule was," Ellis said, "and that I wouldn't be much use to them in the evenings. President Anderson said they understand that, and they thought it would still work out." He paused. "Josh, I told him I'd do it."

"That's great, Dad. I'm proud of you. Who's the new bishop going to be?"

His parents looked at each other. "Now, Josh, you have

to promise not to say anything until after sacrament meeting. The new bishop will be Paul Baxter."

Josh's mouth dropped open. "You're kidding."

In sacrament meeting that afternoon the new bishop was asked to say a few words. He seemed overwhelmed. "I don't know much about being a bishop," he began. He stopped and looked over the congregation before continuing. "But I do know I can't do it alone. Everyone will have to get involved. I also want to tell you that I couldn't do this without Marilee at my side. She's my best friend, and I love her and my children so much."

After sacrament meeting was over, the members of the bishopric and their families met in the bishop's office, where the new bishop and his counselors were set apart. Josh listened to the blessings given to each of them. It seemed to him that these men were somehow different after they were set apart.

As they were about to leave, Bishop Baxter asked Josh, "Where was Richard today?"

"His dad said he thought it would be better if they didn't come out to church for a while."

"Why?"

Then Josh told him everything.

The following Wednesday, Josh, Bishop Baxter, and the four boys responsible for pantsing Richard walked slowly up the sidewalk and knocked on the door of the Stegman house. Carol came to the door.

"I'm the one who talked to you on the phone," Bishop Baxter said. "Thank you for letting us come over."

She invited them into the living room, where Dave, Richard, and Nicole were waiting.

The night before, Josh and Bishop Baxter had gone to the home of each of the boys who had been playing basketball at the church the previous Saturday. With the parents in the room, Bishop Baxter asked each boy to describe what had happened. After they visited a few homes, the truth began to emerge. Four boys had been responsible, and now those four boys sat in the Stegmans' living room.

Bishop Baxter introduced the four boys to the Stegmans. "These boys have something they want to say," he explained.

Jeremy Lockwood had taken the lead in pantsing Richard. He was fifteen, but large for his age. His face was red, his eyes a little puffy. He kept his eyes on the floor. "What we did was wrong," he said softly.

"Jeremy, can you speak up? We can't hear you," the bishop said. He was sitting next to Jeremy with his hand on his forearm for support.

"What we did was wrong," Jeremy repeated a little louder. "We won't ever do it again."

Bishop Baxter patted his arm, then turned to the other boys. The next two boys each mumbled an apology. When his turn came, the fourth boy, Scott Parker, was sobbing and had his head down. Richard came over and knelt down so he could make eye contact with him. "Don't cry," Richard said. "It's okay."

Bishop Baxter waited for Scott to gain control. The boys had been told they each had to say they were sorry. Finally Scott blurted out, "I'm really sorry."

Carol went to the bathroom and brought back a box of tissues. She put it on the coffee table in front of the boys. Scott grabbed one and wiped his eyes.

"The boys are sorry for what they did," Bishop Baxter said to Dave Stegman.

"They should be," Dave replied. "There's no excuse for that kind of behavior anywhere, but I don't mind telling you it's real hard for me to see how this can happen in a church."

There was a long, painful silence. The boys looked to the bishop to say something, but he kept quiet.

Finally Carol couldn't stand it any longer. "Dave, they said they were sorry. What more do you want from them?"

"What's your name?" Dave asked, looking at Jeremy.

"Jeremy Lockwood."

"You got a mom and dad?"

"Yes."

"Do you think they care what happens to you?"

"Yeah, they do."

"Do you think I love my son less than they love you?"

Jeremy's lip quivered. "No."

Carol saw what was happening. "Dave, he's only a boy."

Dave ignored her. "You're right. I love my son just as much as your parents love you. Let me ask you a question—how would your parents feel if a group of boys ganged up on you like you boys did to my son?"

Jeremy was betrayed by the tears welling up in his eyes. "They'd be mad."

"That's right, they'd be real mad. Now I know it takes a big man to own up to his mistakes, and so I want you to know I appreciate you boys coming over here, but that doesn't mean that suddenly everything is fine. I'm still mad that my son was attacked at church by people who should have known better."

Jeremy took a tissue from the box on the coffee table and dried his eyes. "We'll make sure it never happens again," he said. "Whenever Richard is at church, we'll stay with him and make sure nobody ever picks on him anymore."

"Dave, please," Carol said. "The boys are trying their best to make it right."

"I know, but it's too little, too late. The thing is, I knew this was going to happen. I knew it was just a matter of time." Dave turned to face the new bishop. "Why is it that my son gets better treatment practically any other place he goes than he gets at your church?"

"Dad, Josh goes to that church too," Nicole said. "So you can't blame the church totally."

"Well, that's right too, I guess. Josh, you're the best thing I've ever seen come from your church."

Richard approached the boys. "Do you want to see my medals for Special Olympics?" he asked.

"Would that be all right?" Bishop Baxter asked Dave.

"Yes, they can go."

Bishop Baxter waited for the boys to go upstairs, then said to Dave and Carol, "I know you're reluctant to have Richard ever come back to church, and I can understand why you feel that way. But if you could just give us a few weeks to teach our members how to be more sensitive to the needs of people like Richard, then I hope you'll let Richard come back."

Dave wasn't convinced. "I'm not promising anything. All we've ever got from you people is empty promises."

Carol wanted to provide cookies for her guests, but her husband told her he thought everyone should just clear out and leave them alone.

In the car on their way home, Bishop Baxter told Josh, "We need to change it so that when Richard walks into church, he feels loved and appreciated, and nobody makes fun of him. You think we can do that?"

"Not really," Josh said.

"Why not? The Savior would never turn anyone away."

"Do you think people at church sit around thinking about Jesus all the time? Well, let me tell you, they don't."

"Maybe that's the problem then."

"Maybe so," Josh said. "The thing is, you don't notice people making fun of Richard at church but I do. You haven't heard people call him a retard behind his back. I'm sorry but I don't have much hope anymore that anything can change."

"We have to try. I need your help, Josh."

Josh couldn't turn down Paul Baxter. "I'll do what I can."

"I'll schedule a ward council meeting. I want you at that meeting, Josh."

Josh felt out of place at ward council, sitting with men and women he had looked up to for so long. Bishop Baxter conducted the meeting. "I've asked Josh to sit in on our meeting today," he began. "Josh is friends with Richard and Nicole Stegman. Nicole goes to high school with Josh. Richard—well, Richard is developmentally disabled. You may remember him singing with the Primary children in sacrament meeting. I'd like Josh to tell us what happened last Saturday."

"Well, Nicole and I brought Richard to the church to play basketball. While he was here, some boys pantsed and then made fun of him."

The bishop said, "Josh and I took the four boys responsible to apologize for what happened. Richard's father is still pretty bitter about it. I guess something like this happened just after the Stegmans were baptized. I doubt if they had been in the church long enough to gain a strong testimony. What I'm hoping is that Richard will be allowed to come back to church in a few weeks. Before then we need to learn how to deal with those who are different. And so what I'm hoping we can do today is come up with a plan that will help us get ready for when Richard comes back." He paused and looked around the room. "Now I know that not everyone may agree that this is something we should be doing. So I guess I need to know how you feel."

There was a long silence.

"Please feel free to express what is in your heart," the bishop said.

The Primary president raised her hand. "Bishop, you saw how disruptive the boy was during the Primary children's program. The children worked very hard on that program."

"Yes, I know they did."

"I felt bad for the children," she said.

"Of course you did."

"If he comes back, who's to say something like that wouldn't happen again?" the elders quorum president asked.

"I guess we can't guarantee it won't happen again," Bishop Baxter said.

Josh wanted to stand up and tell them they were all wrong to question the bishop, but he didn't because these men and women were people who had been his teachers and leaders. Besides that, he knew how strongly the bishop felt about making changes in people's attitudes and yet how much he was willing to let people speak their mind. And so Josh kept his peace and offered a silent prayer that things would turn out all right.

The Relief Society president spoke next. "My sister has a daughter like Richard," she said hesitantly. "She can be a handful at times, but my sister says they feel very blessed to be her parents. I think most of us just haven't had much experience with children like this. We can learn though. I'm confident of that."

"Thank you," the bishop said. "Let's hear from the rest of you."

Brother Sprague, the high priests group leader, slowly rose to his feet and said, "I know some were offended to have Richard up there singing with the Primary. The boy has the loudest singing voice I've ever heard." He smiled and pointed to his hearing aid. "Even I could hear him." The group appreciated the humor.

"I think it's perfectly reasonable to ask who else was offended," he continued, "but I think we need to start at the top. Was Heavenly Father offended? Was the Savior offended?" There was silence in the room. "I don't think so," he went on. "The boy wasn't being sarcastic or rude. Of course, he wasn't being shy either, but I guess that's just the way he is. The way I look at it, it wouldn't hurt us to try to be more open to people with special needs. If the Savior wouldn't turn these people away, why should we?"

"Thank you very much, Brother Sprague," Bishop Baxter said. "Josh, we haven't heard from you."

Josh took a deep breath and then slowly spoke. "I know it might seem hard to believe—I know it was for me when I first met Richard—but Richard really has a lot to offer. I think we should go along with what Bishop Baxter wants to do."

"Thank you. Josh has been a great friend to Richard."

Like water seeking its level, the discussion ebbed and flowed until finally there seemed to be consensus. It was only then that the bishop said, "I think we're in agreement then, aren't we? We will move forward to educate our members how to deal with those who are different from us." He opened his Book of Mormon and turned to the seventeenth chapter of Third Nephi. "If the Savior could say to the Nephites, 'Have ye any that are sick among you? Bring them hither. Have ye any that are lame, or blind, or halt, or maimed, or leprous, or that are withered, or that are deaf, or that are afflicted in any manner? Bring them hither and I will heal them, for I have compassion upon you'—if the Savior could say that then, is he any less concerned about such people today? Those whom the Savior loves, we must love also. From your comments, I feel assured that by working together we can make a difference."

Josh looked at his father, wanting to know how he felt about all this. But his father said nothing.

Josh went to Nicole's house after the meeting and returned home at eight that night. As soon as he walked into the house, his father said he wanted to talk with him. They sat in the kitchen. His father looked more uncertain of himself than Josh had ever seen him. "All my life," he began, "I've tried to fulfill whatever callings I received in the church and to honor my priesthood leaders. It was the way I was taught when I was growing up. But after our meeting today, I'm not sure where I fit in. I've never felt comfortable with people like Richard. You know what I think? You're the one who should have been called to be the bishop's counselor, not me."

"I can't be his counselor, Dad, you know that."

"I know. The problem is, I'm not sure I can either."

"You can change, Dad, I know you can."

"As you get older, it becomes harder to change. I might need some help from you."

"In what way?"

"I need you to teach me . . . " His voice broke, and it was a few moments before he could continue. "Teach me to learn to . . . deal with . . . people like Richard."

Josh reached out and laid his hand on his father's arm. "The main thing with Richard," he said, "is that you just have to spend some time with him. He's got a lot to offer."

"He does? What?"

"Well, he's always happy. And I really like the way he smiles when he sees me. There're a lot of good things you can get from being around people like Richard. There's nothing as wonderful as being hugged by him when he first sees you. He's taught me a lot about hugging."

"Yes, but I've never been comfortable with hugs."

"I know," Josh said. "Why is that?"

"I guess it's just the way I was brought up."

"You can change."

"I'm not sure I can."

"You can, Dad, I know you can. Why don't you start coming with me to Special Olympics? You could help out like I do."

"I can't go to Special Olympics at three o'clock and do a weather report at five-thirty."

"Why not? It's only once a week," Josh said.

"Because that's my busiest time. I have to get ready."

"Can't you prepare ahead of time? The weather doesn't change that much in a couple of hours, does it?"

"People don't want to know what the temperature was two hours ago."

"Okay, you could work at Special Olympics from three to four and then you'd still have some time to get everything ready."

"I'm already under a lot of pressure because of the Weather Girls. If I start taking time off, it's not going to look good to my boss."

"At least come one time to see what it's like. You can get the guy who does the weather weekends to fill in for you. Okay?"

"We'll see."

The next week Ellis went with Josh to the Special Olympics practice. He wore a Forty-Niners sweatshirt and jogging shoes and carried with him a clipboard that held a yellow legal pad and a pencil tied to a string. Josh wasn't sure what his father thought he was going to do with it, especially since his time was so limited. The most he could spare was an hour, and then he needed to get to the studio to update the visuals he would use.

They arrived early, even before Brandy Wilson.

"What kind of work does Brandy do?" Ellis asked Josh.

"She's an accountant."

"Who does she work for?"

"I don't know. What does it matter?"

A car pulled up. A woman got out, went to the passenger side, opened the door, and helped her daughter, a girl about twelve years old, out. The girl's left wrist was bent down and immovable. She could barely walk. Josh ran over to her and said, "Amanda, how you doing today?"

Amanda smiled and said something. Josh knew it was hello, but he knew his father could not have understood.

"Amanda, guess what? I brought my dad with me today. You want to meet him?"

His father came forward.

"Dad, this is Amanda. Amanda, this is my dad. Dad, Amanda is twice as fast a runner as she used to be. Isn't that great?"

"Hello, Amanda. I'm glad to meet you," Ellis responded.

Brandy Wilson arrived next, and Josh introduced her to his father. She then excused herself to go set up the equipment. As the other children came, some of them recognized Josh's father as the one who did the weather on TV. They felt he was a friend they already knew.

"All right, everybody," Brandy called out. "I think we're ready to start."

"Are we going to have uniforms?"

"Yes, we're going to have uniforms. I'm working on it. Okay, now listen up. We're going to have you practice running again today. Josh's dad, Mr. Dutton, is going to record your times. Josh is going to help you guys with the baseball toss."

As the runners crossed the finish line in their practice runs, Ellis tried to say something positive about each one's effort. Every comment was personalized. He seemed to relax more as time went on. Watching his father reminded Josh of how important Ellis's encouragement had been to him all the way back to when he was on a sixth-grade basketball team.

At the end of the practice, Brandy Wilson asked Ellis, "You going to come back next week?"

"Yes, I'll be back. Maybe only for an hour, but I'll be back."

When it came to adults, Brandy was not one to pile on a lot of praise. "Fine," she said. "Keep the stopwatch then."

Friday night Bishop Baxter and Josh visited Dave and Carol Stegman's home.

"Thank you for letting us come," Bishop Baxter said as they sat down in the living room. "I wanted to let you know what we've done to try to prepare for Richard coming back to church."

"All right."

"We've visited every class and talked to them about how important it is that every person who comes to church feels welcome. In our priesthood and Young Women lessons, we've tried to educate our youth so they'll be more sensitive to those who aren't the same as them. I've asked the older boys to make sure that Richard is made to feel welcome. We've met with the adults and tried to explain why the Savior taught about a shepherd who left the ninety and nine in safety and concerned himself with one who was gone. The response of our people has been excellent. In fact, I've asked our stake president if our ward might be also designated for the learning-impaired and wheelchair-bound members of our stake. This represents not just a temporary effort for us. It is a total, long-term commitment. We'll do whatever we need to do to make worship for all our members a sweet experience. We'd like Richard and you two, and, of course, Nicole, to attend church from now on."

"You've gone to a lot of trouble for one boy," Dave Stegman said.

"Some people have told me that," the bishop replied.

"How have you answered them?"

"Would it be too much trouble if it were your son?"

Dave nodded. "I guess we'll risk letting him start going again."

"What about you and your wife? We'd be honored if you'd come too."

"We're not much when it comes to going to church."

"Good. That's just the kind of people we're looking for."

"If you came, I know my mom and dad would want to have you over for dinner afterwards," Josh said.

Dave turned to Carol. "What do you think?"

"It probably wouldn't kill us to go at least once."

Dave smiled. "Yeah, true, but I'm thinking if we hold out a little longer they'll throw something else in the deal besides just a meal."

Carol, who didn't know Paul Baxter well enough to know if he had a sense of humor, said, "What Dave's saying is, it looks like we'll be out on Sunday."

The services that Sunday weren't perfect; nothing ever is. But they were better. The Stegman family sat in the main section of the chapel, and Richard seemed to be more calm with his parents on either side of him. After sacrament meeting, he attended a special Sunday School class made up of youths his age who had volunteered to be with him. Jeremy Lockwood was now his protector and friend.

After church the Stegmans and the Duttons got together for the first time.

"Real nice place you've got here," Dave Stegman said as soon as he sat down in the Duttons' living room.

"Thank you," Jeanine Dutton said.

"You ever think about doing any remodeling?"

"Dave, that's enough," Carol warned. "You're not here to sell a remodeling job."

"All I did was ask a simple question."

"Well, as a matter of fact, we have thought about remodeling," Ellis said.

"What did you have in mind doing? I might be able to give you a few ideas."

"All we've got so far are dreams," Jeanine explained. "Any remodeling we do will have to wait a while. Our daughter, Kristen, is on a mission. And then there's Josh's college and mission."

"If he was mine, I'd throw him out the day after he graduates from high school."

"Is that what you're going to do with me?" Nicole challenged.

"I haven't decided what to do about you yet."

Just before they ate, it was time for the early news. Josh's father asked if they minded watching the Channel Seven Weather Girls.

"They're not half as good as you are," Dave Stegman said after the weather report was over.

"Thank you."

"I watch you every night—" Dave smiled "—except when Carol is out of the house, and then of course I watch the Weather Girls."

Carol and Nicole both threw a couch pillow at him. Dave loved it.

"Just kidding, just kidding. Gosh, can't anyone take a joke around here?"

Jeanine said, "We don't joke about them much. They've taken a chunk of Ellis's audience. And, of course, they don't know a thing about weather. Last night one of them said, 'Sunrise tomorrow will be in the west at five-forty A.M.' "

"So they were off a minute, right?" Dave said, playing dumb.

"The sun rises in the east," Jeanine, who still wasn't used to Dave, responded.

"Nicole, pay attention. I know this is new information for you," Dave teased. Then he added, "My daughter has never seen a sunrise."

"That's because you never let me stay up that late," she said.

"No, actually, some people get up early."

Nicole kissed her father on the cheek and commented, "What a strange thing to do."

"Where have I gone wrong?" Dave lamented.

After they ate, Richard played a video game in the TV room while Josh and Nicole sat on the couch a few feet behind him and watched. Josh put his arm around her and she snuggled next to him. "You think we'll ever get married?" he asked.

"I don't know. Maybe so . . . someday."

"Let's pretend like we've been married for a couple of years and we've come home to show off our baby," he said.

"Is our baby a boy or a girl?" she asked.

"A boy."

"I want it to be a girl," she said.

"Okay, it's a girl. Our parents are playing with our baby while we're resting. And you should see Richard. He's the proudest uncle you've ever seen."

"What is Richard doing these days?" Nicole asked.

"He has a job."

"Where?"

"He works at Wal-Mart, stocking shelves," Josh said. "He lives in an apartment near the store. He's seeing a girl he met at a Special Olympics meet. They're kind of serious."

"He's happy, isn't he?"

"Yes, very. Things have turned out all right for him."

"I'm glad. We're happy too, aren't we?" she whispered in his ear.

"Yes."

The steady sound from the video game began to blend into the background.

"What are we doing now?" she asked a few minutes later.

"We're falling asleep."

"Yes, we are."

They dozed until Richard turned around, saw them asleep on the couch, and tickled their noses.

The state Special Olympics meet took place at a high school track in the state capital the next week. Ellis was able to get away because he talked the station into letting him do a remote at the meet. He and Jeanine sat with the Stegmans in the stands, which were filled with parents, friends, and families, along with volunteers assigned to cheer for individual runners and to see how much excitement they could generate. Josh and Nicole stood at the finish line to cheer on runners from their local team.

Some contestants ran well; some could barely walk. For that one brief moment it didn't matter. They were all winners. Cheers were as loud for the first to cross the finish line as for the last.

One runner—her legs bent and misshapen, her arms withered and weak, her head contorted by spasms—barely hobbled. By the time all the others had finished, she still had nine-tenths of the race yet to run. The support and love from every person focused on that one girl as she, with great difficulty, continued moving.

Josh and Nicole, along with twenty or so others, stood at the finish line and cheered her on. Every step was an

Everest to climb, every breath a challenge. Josh watched her intently as she concentrated, her mind sharp and alert, sending messages to muscles that obeyed only poorly. She drifted out of her lane, but that didn't matter. What mattered was that she was coming closer to the finish line. For one thousand people who were now standing up and shouting out encouragement and love, that was all that mattered.

Nicole was in the front row at the finish line when the girl crossed it at last. "You did it! You did it!" Nicole shouted, hugging the girl.

The girl looked up and with great difficulty repeated, "I did it."

Richard won a bronze medal the first day. He was so proud of it that he wore it in the shower that night after his family returned to their motel.

The next weekend Josh competed in the state finals high school track meet, held in a town in the eastern part of the state. He stood on the sidelines and watched Kevin compete in the discus. There was never any question who would win.

"Good job," Josh said after it was over.

"Thanks. When do you run?"

"Two o'clock."

"They say Sloan has gotten better."

"I've heard that too."

"You know, it's really too bad about you," Kevin said. "Everyone had big hopes for you this year, but what have you done?"

"I've won all but two of the races I've been in."

"Last year you won every race. You're going backwards. Oh well, sure, you've done other things. You've wiped the noses of kids that nobody else cares about. That may impress your band chick, but it doesn't cut it with me. And it doesn't cut it with Sloan. He's a machine, and all he thinks about is winning. That's why you're going to lose today."

"I'm not going to lose today. I spend my time with kids who give all they've got in every race they run. For some of them, even walking is tough. I've learned more from those kids than anybody else. I'm going to put as much effort into my race as they do in theirs. That's why I'm going to win today."

"Gosh, you really touched me with that little speech," Kevin sneered. He started to walk away, then turned back and said, "It doesn't matter what you say, Josh, it matters what you do. I'm putting my money on Sloan today."

That afternoon Josh competed in the 800-meter race, which required two laps around the track. After half a lap, he was where he wanted to be, just behind Sloan. Sloan glanced around and saw him and sped up to get away. Josh kept up with him.

By the time they completed the first lap, the field had faded back, and it was just Sloan and Josh in contention for first and second. Josh's coach yelled out his time as he completed his first lap. It was his personal best for the first half. Sloan glanced back again at him, put on another burst of speed. Josh matched it.

With half a lap left, Josh kicked out into a sprint, caught up with Sloan, and matched him step for step until they rounded the curve to the finish line. He ran as fast as he could, concentrating on making each step count, each leg contribute the same.

Josh crossed the finish line just one step ahead of Sloan.

10

On the first week in June, Josh and Nicole graduated from high school. That night both sets of parents hosted an open house for them at Nicole's house. By eleven-thirty everyone had left, and Josh and Nicole changed into sweats so they could shoot baskets in the driveway.

She made a basket from free-throw range.

"You've gotten better since you've started tagging along with me," he said.

"Or else you've gotten worse."

"Not likely." He shot, and the ball swished through the net. "I'm glad we got together."

"Me too, Josh."

"You've been good for me, I think."

"Yes, I have, Josh. And it's really paying off. I mean, look how good you're turning out."

"I suppose you take full credit for it too, don't you?"

"Absolutely. Just think, if this is what I can do in a few months, just think what I could do if I had . . . well, you know, an even longer time."

"You were going to say eternity, weren't you?" he teased.

"No, I was not going to say eternity."

"Don't give me that. You were—you know you were. The reason you didn't is because you were afraid I'd get nervous if you talked about us, you know, getting married someday."

"I'm not going to worry about it. If we get married after your mission, fine. If we don't, then, hey, no problem, it's your loss."

"My loss? Wait a minute, why is it my loss? Why can't it be your loss?"

Richard came out of the house wearing pajamas and tennis shoes. "Can I play?" he asked.

"It's late," Nicole said.

"Not too late for me."

"Hey, Richard, how about if I keep passing you the ball and you shoot, okay?" Josh said.

"Okay. You're so good to me, Josh."

"That's 'cause I love you."

"I love you too. And Nicole loves you too, don't you, Nicole?"

"Yeah, I guess so, once in a while."

"She's just teasing you, Josh. She loves you all the time. You should get married and have babies and I'll be your uncle."

"Sounds good, Richard, but not for a while. I want to go on a mission first."

"I want to go on a mission too," Richard said.

"You'd be a good missionary too, Richard, because you're not afraid to talk to anyone," Josh said.

"I want to go to Disneyland on my mission."

"I bet you'll do it, too," Josh agreed.

"I will too. You'll see," Richard said.

Richard made two baskets in a row. "Way to go, Richard!" Josh shouted. "You're the only one in your family that has any athletic ability."

"Hey, wait one minute here, what about me?" Nicole protested.

"Like I said, Richard, you're the only one in your family with any athletic ability."

"I can beat you in a race anytime," Nicole said.

"Richard, do you think she can beat me in a race?"

"No way. Nicole, you're in big trouble if you think you can beat Josh."

"He's not that fast. Whataya say, hotshot, you want to race me right now?"

"Anytime."

"Okay, we'll race down to the end of the block and back again. Richard, your job is to start us off and then you say which one wins." They moved into the street. "Okay, Richard, you count to three and then say go."

"One . . . "

Nicole got down on her knees.

"What are you doing, praying?" Josh teased.

"Two . . . "

She reached over and untied one of Josh's shoes. "Oh, sorry. Here let me help you."

He backed away. "Get away from me."

"I just want to tie your shoe for you. What's the matter, don't you trust me?"

"I've never trusted you," he told her.

"Why not?"

"Three . . . " Richard called out.

"Because you have a serious character flaw," Josh said.

"Three means go," Richard said.

"Character flaw?" she objected. "My only character flaw is that I spend too much time with you. Look, are we going to race or not?"

"We'll race when I'm ready to race—after I tie my shoe." He bent down to tie his shoe.

"I feel bad now that I untied your shoe," she said as she leaned on him, trying to push him over.

"You should." He moved away, finished tying his shoe, and stood up. "Okay, I'm ready now. C'mon, let's race."

Nicole started speaking like a TV sports announcer. *"Josh Dutton . . . the man . . . the legend. . . . What can you say that would ever do justice to his phenomenal high school sports career? Who would have thought it would all be dashed in pieces by the Stegman Factor? Yes, that's right, Nicole Stegman, the fastest woman in the world, totally humiliated Dutton on the night of his graduation. He was never the same after that. He could not bear the shame of being beaten by, of all things, a trumpet player. After that, he spent the rest of his life hanging around street corners chasing cars and barking at full moons."* She howled like a coyote.

A porch light came on across the street, and man in a robe came out. "What's going on there?" he called out. "People are trying to sleep."

"Sorry," Nicole said. "I tried to tell my friend here not to make so much noise. Look, if you want to report him, his name is Josh Dutton. That's D-u-t-t-o-n. I can give you his address, if you want."

"What are you talking about?" the man said. "You were the one that was making all the noise."

"Oh, really? Sorry about that, sir. This is our graduation night. It only comes around once, you know. We're going to stay up all night."

"Go somewhere else. I'm trying to sleep."

"We will. Sorry." She and Josh and Richard started back to the house. "I guess I told him off," she said.

"Yeah, right. 'Sorry, sir . . . yes, sir . . . no, sir.' No doubt about it, all right, you really put him in his place."

"Who cares anyway? Let's not race, okay? There's no point in it. You'd just win again. Besides, tonight is for fun. Richard, are you having a good time?"

"When Josh comes over, I have a good time. Josh is my friend."

"What about you, Nicole?" Josh asked. "Do you have a good time when I come around?"

"It's okay, I guess," Nicole said. "It's not all that great, you understand, but I'd give it a rating of fair . . . average . . . run of the mill . . . nothing to brag about . . . ordinary . . . a little boring—but other than that, not too bad."

"She means it's been her best time too," Richard said.

"Thanks for telling me," Josh said.

"All right, you guys, we're going to stay up all night, okay?" Nicole said. "At least until the sun comes up. That way we'll always remember graduation night. You two won't fall asleep on me, will you? All my life I've wanted to stay up all night with my friends, and I never have because they always wimp out on me."

"What's so great about staying up all night?" Josh asked.

"It's like saying to the world, 'The rules of life don't apply to me.' "

"What are we going to do until the sun comes up?" Josh asked.

"We could watch a movie," Nicole said. "But we can't fall asleep."

"Let's watch *Beauty and the Beast,*" Richard said.

"Gosh, Richard, we've seen that so many times. Isn't there something else you'd like to see?"

"No. You're the Beauty and Josh is the Beast."

They went in to the family room and started the movie. Ten minutes later Richard was asleep at one end of the couch, and Josh, at the other end, was losing the fight to stay awake.

Nicole snuggled up close to him. "Josh," she said softly in his ear, "wake up."

"What?" he droned.

"You're falling asleep. You're not supposed to do that. We're going to stay up all night, remember?"

"Uh . . . huh," he mumbled. Having her so close to him woke him up, but he kept his eyes closed and didn't move.

"Josh, are you awake?" she whispered.

He didn't say anything.

"Josh, this is our graduation night," she said softly. "We'll never be in high school ever again. Josh, can you hear me? You can't, can you? All right then, I want to say some things I'd never be able to say to you when you were awake, but I can tell you now because you're asleep."

With that Josh became wide awake, but he kept his eyes closed.

"Josh, I'll never love anyone like I love you," she went on. "You've been my very best friend. Thank you for being so good with Richard. I judge guys by the way they treat Richard, and you've been so good to him. I want to thank you for that. Sometimes I wish your mission were over. I know we're going to be away from each other for a while. That's going to be hard for me, but I know you have to go away to get stronger. I have to grow strong too."

She was resting her head on his shoulder.

"I love to be close to you like this. No other guy interests me, Josh, only you. I love your face. Sometimes it's a little boy's face and then other times it's so strong and powerful. You know that story about Sleeping Beauty, where the handsome prince comes along and kisses Sleeping Beauty and then she wakes up from a deep sleep? Well, the way it really happened was there was a Sleeping Prince, and the most beautiful girl in the kingdom—her name was Nicole—she came along and saw him, and she fell in love with him and she knelt down and kissed him like this."

She kissed him lightly on the lips. "Josh, you're supposed to wake up now. Hmmmmm . . . maybe the first kiss didn't work. Gosh, maybe I'll have to keep doing this all night until I get it right."

His lips curled into a slight smile. The next thing he knew he was being hit with a couch cushion.

"You big faker, I saw that smile. You were awake all the time, weren't you!"

He opened his eyes as if he were just waking up. "What happened? Who hit me?"

"Don't give me that. You heard everything I said, didn't you!"

"How could I hear you? I was sleeping."

"You weren't sleeping. You knew what was going on. You'd have let me kiss you all night, wouldn't you?"

He tried to be serious, but it was no use. "Gosh no! What kind of a person do you think I am?"

"You no good faker!" She threw another couch cushion at him. "Okay, just for that, buster, you and I have to go outside and do something really dumb."

"Like what?"

She thought about it. "We're going to write on the sidewalk in front of the school, 'Bach Rules the World.' "

"Why would we want to do that?"

"Because it's a dumb thing to do," she said. "I've never been much for dumb things. This is my last chance. C'mon, it's not like it's going to do any damage. The next rain will wash it all away. Don't you see? In high school you can get away with dumb things. I mean, if we were caught, they'd say, 'Writing with chalk on the sidewalk in the middle of the night? What a dumb thing to do.' And we'd say, 'Yes, sir, it was dumb, but it wasn't destructive, and besides, what do you expect from us? I mean, after all, we're in high school.' And then they'd let us go. But you mess up once in college and they kick you out. So this is our last chance to do dumb things, but we've got to do it tonight, because tomorrow we'll be responsible adults. C'mon, Josh, we just have until sunrise, but there's still time. Get up, get up, get up." She prodded and pushed until finally he got up.

They found a box of chalk in Richard's room, and fifteen minutes later they stood on the sidewalk in front of the high school. By then Josh was so sleepy that all he could do was respond to her directions. He had thought they would finish in five minutes, but she wanted this to be a work of art, a monument to her high school years. He worked for as long as he could, but eventually he fell asleep on the sidewalk. At some point during the night she rolled him over onto the lawn because he was lying on the place where she needed to write the word *world*.

She finished just before sunrise, woke him up, and made him look at her artwork and tell her how wonderful it was. Then they walked back to the car.

"Can I go to bed now?" he mumbled.

"Yeah, we're done. Is it okay if I take you home and then drive your car to my place? You look too tired to drive."

He nodded his head.

"Josh, thanks for being such a good sport. Right now I have to get some sleep and then look for a job. It's over, Josh. As of right this instant we're adults. There's no stopping us now."

Josh tripped going up the steps to his house. He could hear Nicole laughing hilariously at him as she drove away.

That summer Josh's sister, Kristen, returned from her mission. The two of them had not been close before, but now, with Josh so close to serving his own mission, he felt a special bond with her. He was pleased that she and Nicole got along so well.

Josh's grandparents on his mother's side came to hear Kristen report on her mission in sacrament meeting. They had by then gotten over the fact that Josh didn't want to go to the university they had picked out for him.

For Josh that summer was his best, not only because he got to be with Nicole every day, but also because he worked for Stegman Construction. He grew to love the smell of sawdust. Wood in any form was something to be worked with and coaxed into becoming something wonderful. He came to be trusted enough by the other men Dave Stegman hired that they would tease him unmercifully. They sent him on errands to hardware stores to pick up tools that were impossible to find or didn't exist. They accused him of dating the boss's daughter just so he could take over the company some day. He told them that it was true, and that when it happened he was going to fire them all.

There were some jobs during the summer that Dave Stegman reserved for Richard. Richard loved working for his dad and getting paid. Most of the time when he was on the job, Josh was asked to work nearby and keep a close watch. Josh didn't mind at all.

During the summer Richard began to have seizures more often. At first the doctors thought it was some kind of allergic reaction to all the dust around construction sites. But even when he stayed home for a week, the seizures continued. Tests were run but they were inconclusive. And then the seizures stopped.

In the middle of July, after a Special Olympics practice, Brandy Wilson asked Josh and his father and Nicole to come to her apartment for some of her birthday cake. Josh could never turn Brandy Wilson down. He said yes before the others, even if they had wanted to, could gracefully back out.

Brandy lived in a small apartment on the fourth floor of a walk-up apartment building. Josh looked around the apartment. She didn't have much furniture, and most of what she had was old and worn. He knew what she did with her money: she used it for whatever she needed for Special Olympics.

"Sorry, I don't have any candles," she said as she cut the cake at a card table in the living room. "Don't anyone ask how old I am, okay?" She slid the pieces onto paper plates and handed one to each of them.

"Brandy?" Josh said.

"What?"

"I love you."

She busied herself with cleaning up a few crumbs from the table.

"I love you too," Nicole added, "for what you've done for my brother."

Brandy turned away. "Stop," she said. "I didn't bring you up here for that kind of nonsense."

"We all love you, Brandy," Ellis Dutton said. "If it weren't for you, nothing would have ever happened with all those Special Olympics kids."

She picked up a napkin and wiped the knife she had used to cut the cake. "Those kids are . . . everything to me," she muttered.

"Come over here and sit down," Ellis said. "We need to talk."

"What about?"

"I know a few people around town. I think we need to get them together to see what we can do to help you."

By the time they left Brandy's apartment, they had worked out a plan. The next week Ellis and Brandy began visiting service clubs telling about Special Olympics and asking for support. By the time school started in the fall, they had raised enough money for uniforms and some operating expenses for the next year.

11

That fall Josh and Nicole enrolled as freshmen at State College, an hour's drive away. They rode together each day.

College was a more difficult transition for Josh than for Nicole. In high school he was popular; in college nobody knew him. In high school he got good grades without studying; in college, he had to work hard just to get a C.

For Nicole, just the opposite occurred. In high school, although she was first-chair trumpet player in the band, nobody paid much attention to her. But at State, she soon became known in the music department as a highly gifted musician. She was given a scholarship after the university symphony director heard her play once. She was the only freshman in the college's brass ensemble.

Because Josh and Nicole were changing, their relationship had to change too.

"Want to go out and shoot a few baskets?" Josh asked one Saturday morning.

"Not really," she said. "I've got other things I'd rather do. Shooting baskets is your thing, Josh, not mine. If you want to, go ahead. If you want to know the truth, it's not that much fun for me to stand around and go, 'Oh, good shot, Josh.' "

"You never complained about it before."

"That's right, I never did."

"Are you saying you never enjoyed it?" he asked.

"Sometimes I did, but not always."

"I didn't know that." He paused. "What do you want to do then?"

"I want to listen to a Wynton Marsalis tape. You're welcome to join me."

"You've changed."

"The way I understand it, that's what we're supposed to do in college."

"I suppose. It's not the same between us now, though."

"Maybe that's because to you the only acceptable role for a woman is to be a cheerleader," she said.

"Oh my gosh, Nicole, that's not true."

"Oh, you mean I can have a life too? Fine. Then come and listen to some music with me."

"No."

"Why not? Why do I have to be the one who always goes along with your plans?"

Josh's first reaction was to answer, "Because you're a girl." But he was smart enough to hold his tongue. He decided that until he understood better what she was saying, he'd better not make her angry. So he went outside and shot baskets with Richard.

Ten minutes later Richard said, "Let's go ask Nicole to play with us."

"I've already asked her. She doesn't want to."

"I'll go ask her."

"It won't do any good," Josh called out as Richard went inside.

A couple of minutes later Nicole came out with Richard.

"What's the deal here?" Josh asked as they took turns shooting baskets. "You won't come out for me but you will for Richard?"

"That's right."

"How come?"

"That's just the way it is. Richard and I are buddies. Isn't that right, Richard?"

"That's right. We are best buddies."

From this Josh began to understand that no matter how Nicole changed for him, she chose to stay the same for Richard. She would always be there for Richard no matter what changes occurred in her own life. She would never let herself grow apart from her brother.

"Do you ever flirt with girls in your classes?" Nicole asked one night as they drove home.

"No, why?"

"Well, you talk to other girls, don't you?" she asked.

"Yes."

"Do you ever flash 'em your sexy smile?"

"Sometimes I smile, yes, I do, I admit it. Whether or not it's sexy, you'd have to ask them."

"Do you ever ask a girl for her phone number?" she asked.

"No."

"I think you should sometime."

"Why?"

"Because I don't think it's good for a person to be stuck in the same old routine all the time."

"All right," he said, "what's his name?"

She hesitated before answering. "Cameron Benning."

"With a name like that he's got to be a music major, right?"

"Yes. He plays the violin."

"You have such a weakness for musicians. How old is he?"

"He's my age but he's brilliant. When he was in high school, he won a young artist competition and played a piece with the Grand Rapids Symphony. He says I'm the best trumpet player my age he's ever heard."

"I'd say that too if I were him."

"You don't think it could be true though, do you?"

"You're very good, anyone can see that."

"He asked me to have dinner with him on Friday night," she said.

"Are you going?"

"Yes, I am."

"Fine, that's just great," Josh muttered.

Saturday morning Josh was watching cartoons on TV with Richard when Nicole came down the stairs in the sweats she slept in. Her hair looked as if she had stuck her finger in an electrical socket. She didn't know Josh was there until she reached the bottom of the stairs. "Why didn't somebody tell me Josh was here?" she complained on her way back upstairs.

"Josh is here!" Richard called out cheerfully.

"It's too late now, Richard. Next time tell me before I come downstairs, okay?"

"Okay," Richard said.

An hour later she came down again, showered and dressed. She breezed past Josh and Richard and went into the kitchen for breakfast. Josh went in to be with her and to have a sticky bun.

"Why are you always hanging around here?" she snapped.

"Fine, thanks, and how are you?"

"Oh, I'm sorry. I'm in a rotten mood."

"How was your date last night?" he asked.

"It was good about ninety percent of the time."

"Is this a new rating system?"

"I don't have to report my every waking hour to you, do I?"

"No, keep whatever secrets you want."

"There're no secrets. We went to his apartment and had a small tossed salad with his special dressing, and baked flounder, and undercooked green beans, and, let's see—oh, yes, rolls he made himself, and cheesecake that he made from a mix. He's an excellent cook. And then we listened to a recording of him when he performed with the Grand Rapids Symphony. He was seventeen then."

"It's been downhill for him ever since then, right?"

"Josh, give me a break. I'm in no mood for this."

"So ninety percent of the time you spent with him was good. What about the other ten percent?"

She sighed. "That'd be the part where he asked me to spend the night with him."

"You're kidding, right?"

"Nope. He asked. You know how football players talk about being blindsided? Well, that's the way it was for me. One minute we're talking about Wagner, the next minute he says he would really appreciate it if I would stay the night with him."

"What did you tell him?"

"I told him I didn't do that because I was a Mormon. We spent the rest of the time talking religion. And then he took me home." She paused. "Something he said really bothers me. After I said I wouldn't stay the night with him, he said, 'Well, it never hurts to ask.' Can you believe that? Does that mean he asks every girl he goes out with? I couldn't believe it." She sighed. "On the way home, though, we listened to Bach."

"Bach? Well, that must have made everything okay then, right? Are you going out with him again?"

"No, how can I? I'd like to hang around with you for a while, if that's all right. At least I know what to expect from you."

"Sure, anytime. Look, from now on you can count on

me to go with you to any dumb, boring concert you want to go to."

She tilted her head back and laughed. "I can see it now: Josh Dutton, music critic for the *Westmont Gazette*. Every review would begin—" she spoke in her imitation of a male athlete "—'This was really a dumb concert.' "

"I'm serious. Even if you want to go hear some guy in a tux scrape chalk across a blackboard, I'll go with you. Hey, I'll even wear a sport coat. Just say what you want and I'll come through for you. One more thing—I hate to sound stupid, but what the heck is flounder anyway?"

"Flounder is what you did the first time we met," she said, with the smart-aleck smile she reserved just for him.

The last half of fall semester was their best time together. They had finally worked through enough of their differences to be close. They began to accept each other's strengths and weaknesses. They became equal partners who did their best to help and encourage each other. The hour-long drive at the beginning and the end of their day became something they both looked forward to. Besides talking about everything from NFL football to Russian composers, they decided to read aloud a chapter a day from the Book of Mormon. Most of the time she read while he drove, but sometimes she drove and he read. She told him it was the first time she had really read the book.

In November Josh submitted his papers for his mission. His nineteenth birthday was coming up in February. He made arrangements to work for Stegman Construction from the end of fall semester until he left for his mission.

He received his mission call during finals week in December. He and Nicole had been on campus all day, either studying or taking finals, and at five-thirty as he drove into Nicole's driveway, Richard came running out, unable to contain his excitement. "Your mother called! Your mission call came in the mail! It's at home! Let's go see where you're going! I bet it's to the Disneyland Mission, 'cause that's where I'm going on my mission."

He jumped into the car and Josh drove home. "Mom, is it here?" he called out as he burst into the house.

"Yes, it's on the kitchen table."

Josh picked the envelope up as if it were a holy document.

"Open it," Richard cried out.

"We can't open it now, Richard. We have to wait for my dad."

"C'mon, just a little peek?" Richard coaxed.

"Nope, we have to wait."

Josh took Nicole and Richard home for supper, and later all of the Stegmans and Bishop Baxter and his family came over. By the time Ellis Dutton came home, it was quarter to eleven that night. Kristen, who was now in graduate school at Utah State University, called and was waiting to hear the big news.

With everyone gathered in the living room, Josh nervously opened the envelope and slowly read the letter. He was being sent to the Utah Ogden Mission. For one slight moment he was disappointed. All his life, Primary and Sunday School teachers and Aaronic Priesthood advisers had told him, "You might be called anywhere in the world. You never know where you'll be called. It could be to England or India or even Russia."

"Where are you going?" Nicole practically screamed.

Josh decided that if this was where God wanted him to serve, then that's where he would serve. After all, he reasoned, Ogden, Utah, is somewhere in the world.

"Tell us!" Richard shouted.

Josh, even on that sacred occasion, couldn't help but have a little fun with his friends. "I've been called to the Ouu Tay, Oog a Den Mission. It's a new mission. I'm sure that you all remember reading about Ouu Tay, Oog a Den in *Time* magazine, don't you?"

He loved the puzzled expression on Nicole's face. "I should've paid attention in geography," she said. "I hate to show my ignorance, but exactly where is Ouu Tay, Oog a Den ?"

Josh scoffed. "You don't know?" To everyone else, he said, "And she's an honor-roll college student—can you believe that?"

She could tell from his smile that something was up. "Wait a minute. Let me see that letter."

He handed it to her.

"It's the Utah Ogden Mission, you big faker!"

"Oh, really? Gosh, I must have read it wrong."

She punched him in the stomach. It didn't hurt though, because he was expecting it.

Richard, more than anyone else Josh had ever known, loved Christmas—not just that one day, but all of it, the busy malls, the long lines, the congested traffic. He delighted in the intrigue of buying presents and wrapping them so nobody could guess what was in the box. Where others made a list so they could buy everything at one time, Richard would have been happy to go to the mall every day to buy one gift.

At the beginning of the season his parents or Nicole and Josh took him fairly often, but as the season progressed, it became more difficult because his health seemed to be getting worse. His seizures became more frequent and, often, more severe than in past years. His mother took him to doctors and specialists, but the tests they ordered came back inconclusive. She began to search out of the state for someone who could tell her what was wrong.

Three days before Christmas Richard was feeling good again, so he asked Josh to take him Christmas shopping.

He wanted to get one more gift for Nicole. Before they left home, Josh tried to get him to indicate what he wanted to buy. He was worried that walking through the mall would be too tiring for Richard. They ended up deciding on gifts that could be purchased at a discount store.

The store was thronged with last-minute shoppers looking for sale items. Richard became exhausted before they made it to the cosmetics counter, where they were going to get some perfume for Nicole. He was so tired that suddenly he just sat down in the middle of the aisle.

"Richard, you can't sit down," Josh said. "There're too many people here. You'll be in their way."

"I'm tired."

"Excuse me," an angry woman behind them called out.

"He just needs to rest for a minute," Josh explained.

"I need to get through," the woman complained.

"He's been sick lately."

"What do you want me to do about it?" the woman snapped.

It wasn't just one shopper. Three others stood behind her.

Josh asked the woman, "Let me have your cart. I'll put him in it."

"No, I won't give you my cart. They shouldn't let people like him in here this time of year."

"What's wrong with him anyway?" the man behind her asked. "Is he retarded?"

Josh blew up. "Why does everyone think there's something wrong with him? There's nothing wrong with him. You people are the ones who have something wrong with you. He'd never treat you the way you're treating him."

"Josh, you okay?" a familiar voice called out. Josh turned around to see Paul and Marilee Baxter. They had heard him from the next aisle. "What's wrong?" Marilee asked.

"Richard is too tired to walk."

"How can we help?" Bishop Baxter asked.

"If we could put him in a cart, I could push it out to the car."

"I think he's too big to get in a cart," Marilee said, "but we passed some wagons a few aisles down. I'll go get one of them, and you two see if you can get Richard up."

"Hi, Bishop," Richard said, enthusiastic but still weak.

They were able to get Richard up enough so other shoppers could squeeze by.

Marilee showed up a short time later with the only assembled wagon in the store. It was bright red. "Hey, Sport, you want to try this thing out?" Marilee called out.

"Sure, I do."

Once he was in the wagon, Richard wanted to finish shopping. Paul and Marilee went to explain what was going on to the store manager while Josh went with Richard to help him pick out gifts. Twenty minutes later Paul and Marilee helped Josh get Richard out to the car.

The next day Richard was feeling better. By Christmas he was back to his old self again.

When a new semester began in January, Nicole continued on at State College. Josh went to work for Stegman Construction to earn more money for his mission. Though he was working up to sixty hours a week, he continued to help out with Special Olympics whenever he could.

He tried to see Nicole, but because of his long hours, days went by when he didn't see her at all. In February she went on a one-week tour with the college's brass ensemble. When she returned, she was so far behind in her other classes that she had to ration out her time with Josh to short periods at odd hours of the day or night.

Josh felt that Nicole and her family were growing stronger in their testimonies. Her parents didn't go to church every Sunday, but usually they went two or three times a month. They quietly told him they were impressed that ward members still continued in their support and love for Richard. Now every fast and testimony meeting had two things in common. The first was that Richard would stand up and tell people he loved Heavenly Father and Jesus and his mom and dad and Nicole and Josh. And at some time during the meeting one or more people would get up and say how much they loved it when Richard gave them one of his famous hugs.

Whenever Josh looked at Nicole, he thought about how hard it would be to leave her for two years. He had a strong resolve to serve a mission, but it was impossible for him not to notice that she was becoming more beautiful, more fun to be with, more sure of her own worth, more appealing to every guy who saw her. Josh had no fear of guys who looked like him. What he worried about were other music majors. Nicole seemed to have a weakness for men who loved music as much as she did. And as hard as he tried, Josh could never get much beyond country western.

Nicole began to see Cameron Benning once in a while as friends.

"Is he still asking you to spend the night?" Josh asked one day.

"No. We have an understanding about that."

"I don't trust him. Just stay away from him, okay?"

"We're just friends, Josh, that's all. It *is* okay if I have friends while you're gone, isn't it?"

"Sure. Just not him. He's not even a Mormon."

"Who in the music department *is?'*

She was right. There was nobody.

Josh and his family spoke in sacrament meeting the day before they drove him to Utah to enter the Missionary

Training Center. Kristen, now engaged, brought her fiancé to meet the family. In the meeting, Richard sang "I Hope They Call Me on a Mission." He had practiced hard all week so he would do it just right, and his voice was clear and mostly on tune. Even though he wasn't on the program, after he finished his song he went to the pulpit to say a few words. "I love Josh and he loves me," he began. "He's my best friend in the whole world." He looked around at the congregation. "Did you know Heavenly Father is looking down at us right now? Well, he is." Then he looked up. "I'm going on a mission too someday—to Disneyland. Thank you. Amen."

Josh had an appointment with the stake president to be set apart as a missionary half an hour after church. As soon as priesthood meeting was over, he searched all over the building until he found Nicole. "Would you come with me please?" he asked.

He led her into an empty classroom and shut the door. "What's going on?" she asked.

He looked at his watch. "I have seventeen minutes left before I'm set apart as a missionary."

"Yes, I know that."

He was embarrassed to say it, but he confessed, "I won't be able to hug you after I get set apart."

"Oh, Josh, you are such a silly guy." She came to him, and they hugged each other until someone opened the door and hurriedly backed out again. "Oh, sorry."

Josh turned red. "We were just saying good-bye," he called after the man.

"I can go someplace else."

It was over. The time had come. "No, that's okay," Josh said. "We're through here."

The next morning just before Josh and his parents left for Utah, Nicole dropped by the house. She called him

Elder Dutton and shook his hand and waved good-bye as the Duttons drove away.

Josh threw himself into his mission, going after it with the same dedication he had previously reserved only for sports. He received a letter from his parents and one from Nicole once a week. She was busy but enjoying her classes. Six months into his mission she wrote him:

Dear Josh,

Two days ago Richard was admitted to the hospital. The night before, he had one of the worst seizures he's ever had. The doctors aren't quite sure what is happening. I went to see him today, though, and he's a lot better. He asked me to tell you he loves you and that he prays for you every day and night.

I wish you were here. I know he would love to see you. I'm really worried about him. Please pray for him. I know Heavenly Father will listen to your prayers. I'm never that sure about mine.

Love,

Nicole

Two days later she wrote and said that Richard had been released from the hospital and seemed to be doing much better. A few days after that, Josh received a letter from Richard.

Dear Josh,

Did you know I was in the hospital? Well I was. They had cable. After I got better, I watched TV a lot. They had a button that made the bed move. It was fun but they told me to stop. The nurses were nice. I talked to them all the time. They told me to get back in bed. Nicole and I are going to make you chocolate chip cookies. She got the chips. I saw them. Won't you be happy when they come.

I love you. You are my best friend.

Richard

A week later, just as Josh and his companion walked in the door at nine-thirty at night, the phone rang. His companion answered it, spoke briefly, then said, "It's for you."

It was Nicole, sounding devastated. "Josh, something terrible has happened," she sobbed. "Richard died in his sleep last night."

"That can't be. How did it happen?"

"He must have had a seizure. We usually always heard him, but nobody heard him last night."

"I can't believe it," he said, shaking his head.

"Josh, please, I can't go through this by myself. I want you to come home for the funeral. I need you with me. Please come home."

They talked for an hour. As soon as he hung up, Josh phoned home. His mother answered the phone. She told him she had taken food over to Richard's family and had talked to Carol Stegman for a long time. While she was there, Bishop Baxter and his wife had come to make arrangements with the family for the funeral. It would be held three days later.

"Nicole wants me to come home for the funeral," Josh said.

"Is that what you want to do?" his mother asked.

"Yes."

"All right, if that's what you want to do. Do you want me to get a round-trip or a one-way ticket?"

"A round-trip ticket. I'll be coming back to the mission field."

"When will you go back?" his mother asked.

"I don't know. I think that depends on how Nicole is doing."

"If I get you a round-trip ticket, we need to say when you'll be returning."

"Maybe you should just get a one-way ticket then," Josh said.

There was a long pause. "Josh, she has a lot of people here who love her. You're not the only one."

"She asked me to come. How can I tell her no?"

His father, when he got on the line, was more direct. "Are you willing to face the fact that you might not return to your mission after the funeral?"

"I'll come back right afterwards," Josh explained.

"What if Nicole asks you to stay a few weeks?"

"Then I'll stay. What else can I do? You know how much she means to me and how much I cared about Richard. How can I stay out here when they need me at home."

"Richard doesn't need you to come home," his father pointed out.

"Nicole does," Josh said.

"Look, Josh, I know you and Richard were very close, but he's not a member of your family."

"What difference does that make?"

"I don't know. Look, Josh, we'll support whatever decision you make, but before you do anything, please make this a matter of prayer. It's possible that Heavenly Father can bless Nicole and her family more if you dedicate yourself to what you were called to do than if you come home. And please talk with your mission president. It's your decision, and I know you'll do what's best."

Josh went into his bedroom, where his companion, Elder Strom, was asleep. Elder Strom had been in the mission field only two weeks. Josh had been assigned by the mission president to train him. He knew it was an honor to be trusted with a new elder. They had worked hard and now were beginning to see some results. Josh wasn't sure what would happen to Elder Strom if he left to go home for the funeral. He would not be allowed to stay in their area without a companion. In fact, their area would probably be shut down, and the people they were teaching would have to wait. They had three families working toward baptism. What would happen to them?

He tried to imagine what he would do when he got home. He and Nicole would talk about Richard and how much they loved him and what a positive effect he had on people who knew him. They would be together during the funeral, and afterwards he would try to help her understand. More than anything he wanted the comforting influence of the Spirit to let her know that Heavenly Father loved Richard more than anyone else did and that Richard was okay.

He wondered how effective he would be in bringing her blessings if he abandoned his own call to serve God? If he went home, would he ever return to his mission? Nicole wasn't going to get over this in a day or two. He wasn't sure she would ever want him to leave again.

He thought about Richard and wondered what advice he would give. Josh was sure that Richard, if he could, would want to tag along with him as an unseen companion. The thought comforted Josh, and for a brief instant he did feel that Richard was there with him.

After Josh knelt down by the side of his bed and prayed, he knew what he had to do. His brief silent prayer confirmed his decision: he was going to continue on his mission. When morning came, he phoned his mother and asked her to tell Nicole he would not be coming home for the funeral. That night he wrote her a long letter trying to explain why he had decided to stay on his mission.

A week later he received a letter from his mother with details about Richard's death as well as an audiotape of the funeral. She told him that Richard had seemed all right the night before he died. Carol had been sitting on the couch watching TV, and he had come in and lay down with his head in her lap. She had run her fingers through his hair before sending him off to get ready for bed. Sometime during the night he had another seizure. This time it had been quiet and deadly.

The night before the funeral, there was a viewing at the mortuary. Brandy Wilson came. When she looked down into the casket and saw Richard in his Special Olympics uniform with all his medallions around his neck, she stood and sobbed. Dave and Carol Stegman came up to her and hugged her and told her how much Richard loved Special Olympics. Several parents of Special Olympians and some of the teachers who taught Richard in school came. Their mailman came and said that Richard always had a warm hello for him whenever he saw him.

For the funeral the next day, the chapel was full. The Special Olympics team, along with Brandy Wilson, sat together near the front. Bishop Baxter conducted the service. After the Primary children sang "Love One Another" and Marilee Baxter offered the opening prayer, Bishop Baxter asked the team members to stand. He talked about Richard's involvement in Special Olympics and about all the medals he had won. Then he talked about the changes the ward had made to help make Richard feel welcome.

"This wasn't easy for us," he said. "Not everyone even thought it was a good idea. Some would say, is it worth it to change around an entire ward for one person? We know the answer to that question now. The answer is yes. One person is important. Every person is important. Something happened that we had not anticipated. Once we showed we had a commitment to every person's needs, then people began to come forth—people with other kinds of needs, people who felt they didn't want to bother the bishop but who carried scars from things that had happened years ago, people whose marriages on the surface looked good but that were in trouble, people who had been afraid to admit they were in trouble. The lesson we learned is this: when we said that Richard's needs were important, it freed up others to realize that their needs are important too.

"Now that Richard is gone, I hope we won't lose the special feeling we experienced in this ward since he began attending with us. Things may be quieter in our meetings now that he's gone, but they won't be quite the same. I for one will miss him deeply. He showed us that one person can make a difference. We are all of us better people for having loved him. We owe him a debt of gratitude for helping us become more Christ-like. He never had any problem with that, but we did, and he taught us what for him came naturally. I'll never forget him. We need to reach out to anyone else who might be like Richard. That is what Richard would want us to do."

When the funeral procession drove to the cemetery, the day, which had begun cloudy, became clear and bright. At the end of the long line of cars was Brandy's van, filled with members of the Special Olympics team. After the grave was dedicated, everyone, including these special friends of Richard's, returned to the ward for a dinner prepared by the Relief Society and to share their memories of Richard.

Two weeks passed before Josh received another letter from Nicole. She wrote:

Dear Josh,

I know I'm supposed to be noble and tell you I understand why you didn't come home for the funeral. I know that's what I'm supposed to say. But I don't feel very noble right now. This is the lowest point of my life, and I'm having to face it without you.

Nothing anyone says gives me any comfort. Everyone tries though. I've been told that I should be happy because now Richard is with Heavenly Father. I've been told that Richard is normal now so I should be happy. Someone tried to tell me that because I know the plan of salvation, I shouldn't feel bad at all that Richard's gone.

None of these lofty words have helped. Do you want to know what has? At the viewing before the funeral some of the boys and girls from Special Olympics laid some of the medals they'd won in the casket, to be buried with Richard. Can you believe they would do that? And they came up to me and threw their arms around me and said they were sorry. And we held each other and we cried. Of all the ones who tried to help, those kids helped the most of all.

I feel like I'm on empty. I go through the routine of each day. I try to keep busy. I can get through the days, but once I get home it starts in all over again. I keep waiting for Richard to give me a hug and ask me how my day has gone. But he's not here anymore. Sometimes I go in his room and just sit there and think about him.

I haven't gone to church since Richard died. It's just too hard for me to force myself to go. I know I should though. I will. Maybe next week.

My mom and dad are just the opposite. They're going every Sunday. They saw the changes the church made to make it good for Richard. So they're doing okay, I guess. They said for me to tell you hello. Bishop Baxter asked them to help the ward continue to work with boys and girls like Richard. They said they'd do what they could.

I'm sorry for being such a boob. Maybe if I'd grown up in the church, I'd have more faith or courage or whatever it takes. But I'm not brave, at least not now. I know you're doing your best to do what God wants you to do, but right now I can't understand why God didn't want you to help me get through this. And what about you? How important am I to you? How could you turn your back on me when I needed you the most?

This must be a really depressing letter for you to read. I'm sorry—but this is the way I feel.

Please keep writing but don't expect me to answer every letter.

Nicole

Josh wrote to Nicole every week. She answered once in a while, but even then, her letters were usually short and only gave brief highlights of her activities in college. She never again wrote about Richard.

Josh's mother wrote and told him that Nicole finally began attending sacrament meetings with her parents, but she often left early.

One of the things that happened as Josh served in the mission field was that he began to appreciate his parents more than at any other time in his life. There were many things that needed to be said, and he took the opportunity to say them in his letters home. He wanted them to know how he now valued what they had done for him when he was growing up. Whatever rifts had existed between him and his father vanished. Josh had gone through much of his teen years embarrassed by what his father did for a living, but that feeling had now given way to admiration and respect.

His parents tried to let Nicole know they valued her. They even had her over for supper a few times. And they reported that, when they could, they always tried to attend her concerts at the college.

While Josh was away on his mission, Channel Three received a grant that would allow his father to take the weather information into local schools. Twice a week Ellis visited an elementary school and taught the children what they needed to know about severe weather. When a tornado struck a nearby community, at least one boy's life was saved because when the red tornado warning appeared at the right top of the screen, he remembered what he had been taught and went to the basement and took shelter under the stairs. When his parents came home two hours later, the house was gone but their son was safe, still waiting under the stairs.

For the first time in his life Josh found the value of asking his parents for advice. As an adult, he had the option of accepting or rejecting the advice, but he appreciated having the advantage of their years in helping him to see all sides of an issue.

Even though he was hundreds of miles away, Josh had finally come home.

12

Elder Josh Dutton sat in a window seat and watched the sprinkler circles dotting the prairie landscape slip past below him. He was twenty minutes from touchdown, two years and four days from the time he left on his mission.

In his mother's last letter, she told him not to expect Nicole to meet him at the airport. "We asked her," she wrote, "but she said she has a concert the night after you get back. The orchestra is going to practice the night you come home and she can't miss that. In fact, she's going to stay with a friend in the dorm that night. She hopes you'll come to the concert with her parents though. But if not, she'll see you the day after."

At the airport to meet him were his parents; his sister, Kristen, and her husband, Brett, and their three-month-old baby girl, Brittany; Dave and Carol Stegman; and Paul and Marilee Baxter and their children. It was a wonderful reunion—except Nicole wasn't there.

At six o'clock the next morning Josh awoke in his room for the first time in two years. Almost as a reflex action he dropped to his knees, said his prayers, and picked up his Book of Mormon. He read in bed for fifteen minutes and then got dressed and took a walk. He passed Nicole's house even though he knew she wasn't there. The first thing he noticed was that the basketball hoop had been taken down.

That night Josh went with Nicole's parents to State College to the spring concert of the symphony orchestra. On the way they talked about Richard's death. Josh tried to explain to them why he had not come home for the funeral, and they seemed to understand, but they also made it clear that Nicole still didn't understand.

Josh had heard that Nicole and Cameron Benning were still spending time together. "What's he like?" he asked Dave Stegman.

"He's the kind of person who doesn't have a clue how to change the oil in his car," Dave said. "And, another thing, he talks down to me. To him, the only people who count are other long-hair musicians. He can walk in the house, see me, and not even say hello. Nicole says it's because he's gifted. I say, gifted or not, you don't ignore people. I swear she's getting just as bad."

"They're just friends now," Carol added. "Nicole told me he's living with a girl who plays cello."

"A cello player? If that doesn't beat all. You see what I mean?" Dave shook his head.

"Dave, shush," Carol said.

"Does she ever talk about Richard?" Josh asked.

"No, not much," Carol said. "I told her I thought she needed counseling. You can imagine what she thought of that idea."

They arrived at the auditorium a few minutes before the concert. Members of the orchestra were beginning to take their places and warm up. Josh sat on the edge of his seat, waiting for Nicole to appear. When she walked on stage, she was not what he expected. Her hair was very short. It looked as if she had done it herself, but her mother told him she had paid someone a lot of money to make it look that way. She radiated a self-confident sophistication. She was breathtakingly beautiful, but she wasn't what he remembered.

Dave noticed Josh's reaction. "Kind of scary, isn't it?" he commented. "She's turned into the Ice Queen. She's got the kind of look you see in New York City. But still it's okay, I guess. It's her life, right?"

"Which one is Cameron?"

"The one who's tuning everybody else up."

Josh studied Cameron. His jet-black hair was longer than Nicole's. Josh estimated him to be about six foot one. Every motion he made seemed to be choreographed, practiced, and timed to perfection.

"What do you think?" Dave asked.

"Definitely not a guy to help you remodel a bathroom."

"Probably not, but if he did, I'd lay money he'd end up turning it into the Sistine Chapel."

"You two, hush," Carol Stegman said.

After the concert Nicole rode in the back seat with Josh as her parents headed back to Westmont. In three minutes they had run out of conversation. He told her he had enjoyed the concert. She said thank you. She asked how his mission was. He said fine. And that was it. When he looked over at her, she turned immediately toward him as if challenging his right to admire her.

Carol tried desperately to get some kind of conversation going between them, but her efforts fell flat. It was clear to everyone in the car that Nicole had no use for him anymore.

When they arrived at Josh's home, he said to her, "I'll call you sometime."

"Actually, I'm real busy right now."

"Sure, I understand. I'm talking Sunday in sacrament meeting about my mission."

"I'm sure you are," she said.

"I'd like you to come."

"I plan on being there. I want to know what was so important that you couldn't come home for Richard's funeral."

"Nicole," her mother said.

"What?"

Her mother was tired. "Nothing."

True to her word, Nicole came to sacrament meeting and listened to Josh's report on his mission. After sacrament meeting, he caught her in the hall just as she was about to leave.

"Aren't you staying for the rest of the meetings?" he asked.

"No, the brass ensemble usually practices on Sundays."

"I see. Okay. What did you think about my talk?"

"It was good. I took notes. If you ever give the talk again, I have a few suggestions. Oh, I'm sorry. I shouldn't have said that, should I? I forgot how sensitive you are to criticism. It's just that I've had some speech classes since you've been gone."

"I'd like to see what you wrote."

The back of her program was filled with notes. She handed it to him. "Well, I really need to go now," she said quickly.

"I like your hair."

"Do you?"

"I didn't at first, but I do now."

"Well, that's good, I guess. I didn't do it for you though. I did it for me."

"I know that."

"We used to stare at each other like this for hours at a time, didn't we?" she said.

"Yes."

"That was a long time ago. I'm not even the same person anymore. I really have to go now. I'll see you around sometime."

Josh watched her walk away. He felt that someone he had once loved dearly had been snatched away and replaced with a stranger.

The next morning he woke up at six again, studied the scriptures a few minutes, then drove to State College. He went to the information desk in the student union and looked in a student directory for Cameron Benning's address. It was nearly eight when he knocked on the door. He had to knock several times before Cameron, in silk oriental pajamas, came to the door.

"I'm a friend of Nicole Stegman," Josh explained. "I'm kind of worried about her. I'd like to talk to you about her if I could."

"What's your name?"

"Josh Dutton."

"Oh," Cameron said. "Come in. Let me get dressed."

Josh sat down and Cameron went into the bedroom.

"Who is it?" he heard a woman in the bedroom ask.

"It's that religious fanatic Nicole used to go with."

"What's he doing here?"

"He wants to talk about Nicole."

"Tell him he missed his chance when her brother died."

Cameron came back into the living room, closing the bedroom door behind him. "Can I get you anything? A cup of coffee? Some orange juice?"

"No, thanks. I'm fine. The reason I came is because I'm worried about Nicole. You're her friend. I thought maybe you could help me. How's she doing?"

"As far as her music goes, very well. She's very talented, you know. I'm not sure if you ever realized that. She always told me you didn't. She's one of the most gifted musicians to come out of this college in fifty years. Maybe I shouldn't tell you this, because she doesn't even know it yet, but I just found out that she and I are going to receive a scholarship to study at the Juilliard School of Music for a year." He paused. "Oh, sorry, have you ever even heard of Juilliard?"

"Not really. They must not have much of a basketball team."

Cameron's laugh sounded like a mild cough. "Oh, that's rich. You don't mind if I tell my friends what you said, do you? They'll really be amused."

"Does Nicole talk much about me?"

"Not anymore."

"Is she seeing anyone?"

"Not that I know of."

"I thought that maybe you and she . . . "

"There was a time when that might have happened, but—" he gave a slight turn of his head in the direction of the bedroom "—not anymore: Even if I go to Juilliard, Ashley will come with me. Why do you even ask? Are you hoping to pick up where you left off?"

"I'm concerned about her now more as a friend. I've given up any hope for us, you know, the way it used to be."

"I think that's wise. She couldn't understand why you didn't come back for her brother's funeral. Actually, if you want to know the truth, none of us could understand that either."

"It was a tough decision," Josh said.

"You must be a very devout person to just throw away a friendship like you and she had."

"I felt I'd been called by God to do what I was doing and that my staying there would help Nicole more than if I came home," Josh said.

"Really? You actually thought God would pitch in to take up the slack for you? I hate to disillusion you, but I haven't seen any evidence that happened."

"Do you think she's happy?" Josh asked.

"She's busy, she's successful, but, no, I wouldn't say she's happy."

"Is there anything I can do to help her?"

"Not really. I don't think she wants to have anything more to do with you or your church."

Josh stood up. "Thank you. You've been very kind."

"No problem." They walked to the door. "To tell you the truth, I'm not sure she'll ever fall in love again. Since you've been gone, she's had plenty of chances. Usually she goes out once or twice with a guy and then loses interest. She was crazy for you, but then you let her down. I'm not sure she'll ever risk being hurt like that again."

The next day Josh began working for Stegman Construction. He hadn't realized how much he had missed building houses. He felt as if he had come home to an old friend. Every night around eight-thirty he went over to see Nicole. He would have gone earlier, but she taught trumpet lessons from six to eight. And every night, after her mother or father called to her in her room, she came to the door and told him she was too busy.

This continued for a week, and then finally she told him not to come by anymore.

One day Carol Stegman called and gave him a suggestion. The next night at seven-thirty, he showed up at Nicole's house. Carol let him in. Nicole was just finishing up a trumpet lesson with a student. While he waited, he took the trumpet he had rented from a music store earlier in the day from its case.

Nicole ignored him as she walked out with the boy who had just had a music lesson. "Curtis, you're doing really well," she was saying. "Be sure and practice every day this week, okay?"

When she came back, she looked in Josh's direction and said, "I'm busy."

"Your mother said someone just quit, so you have an open time slot now," he told her. "I want to take trumpet lessons."

"I want serious students."

"I am serious."

"That's hard to believe, but if it's true, I'll give you a list of some other teachers," she said.

"I want you as my teacher, and I'm willing to pay what you charge everyone else."

"What are you trying to prove?" she asked.

"Nothing."

"I don't believe that."

"All right. I'm trying to prove I care about you."

"Do you care fifteen dollars a lesson?"

"Yes. And I'd like to have two lessons a week," he said.

"Why?"

"Because I want to learn as fast as possible. I have a lot to catch up on."

"Two lessons a week would be thirty dollars."

"I'm good for the money. I have a job, you know," he said.

"All right, fine, I need the money. Let's get started. Come with me."

During the lesson she was the ultimate professional. She treated him like someone she had just met. On his way out the door, he asked if he could see her later that night.

"I hardly ever socialize with my students," she replied.

"That's probably because except for me, they're all in junior high."

"True, but I want to maintain a consistent policy."

"Fine. I won't ask again."

"I would appreciate that."

Twice a week Josh had a music lesson from Nicole. He

practiced an hour every day because he knew she didn't think he was serious, and he wanted to prove her wrong.

"Why do you keep doing this?" she asked once after a lesson.

"It's the only chance I have to see you."

"You're wasting your money."

"I don't think so. I'm getting better. Even you have to admit that."

"Maybe so, but I've got to tell you this, Josh, the only progress you're making is on the trumpet." She paused. "There's something you should know. I'm going away next fall to New York City. I'll be gone all next year. Cameron and I have each received a scholarship for advanced study at Juilliard."

"I know, Cameron told me. Cameron and you and the cello player he's living with. I can't stop you from going, but at least talk to me."

"I'd rather not."

"Please."

After a long silence, she finally whispered, "All right."

That night around nine-thirty they ended up at the picnic grounds where Richard had fallen into the reservoir the day Josh met him. They sat on a picnic table and listened to the waves lap up on shore.

"I wish Richard were here," he said. "He'd help us get through this."

"It's best for me if I don't think about him."

"Richard was a part of your life. You can't just pretend he never existed."

"I have my music now. That's enough. I don't need anything else. One time a friend and I were at a music store and we saw someone who reminded me of Richard when he was about eight. This boy was running around from piano to piano, banging on the keys. My friend said they ought to put people like him away. I didn't say anything. I didn't tell him anything about Richard, not one word. That's the kind of person I've become, but I can't help it, because when I think about Richard being gone, I feel so bad I can hardly stand it."

"I miss him too, you know."

"I know you do. You were his best friend. In some ways you were a better friend to him than you were to me. At least you never turned him down when he needed you, like you did me."

"Can I be honest with you?" he asked.

"Yes, of course, if I can have the same privilege."

"I know it was hard for you when Richard died. But you didn't need me. There was help for you all along if you'd taken advantage of it. What you needed the most I couldn't have given you even if I'd come home. You turned away from the only source that could have given you comfort. You quit going to church. You quit reading the scriptures. You quit praying. I know you're mad at me still. But the way I see it, you have only yourself to blame for becoming bitter."

"I've tried to come to grips with what happened but I can't. I just can't understand why God would let him die."

"I've thought a lot about that, and I don't know either. There is something I do know, though. I know that Richard is happy where he's at."

"How do you know that?"

"I don't know. I just do."

"I wish I knew that."

"You can."

"How?"

"Start going to church again."

"You're so predictable, Josh. I mean it. That's your answer for everything, isn't it? Well, the church doesn't work for me. I'm sorry, but it just doesn't."

"What does?"

"You want to know the truth? Nothing."

Josh look at her closely in the pale moonlight and was silent for a few minutes. Then he said, "The Savior knew we'd have heartache. He said, 'Blessed are they that mourn, for they shall be comforted.' He'll comfort you if you ask. I know He will. Just give it a try for a while, okay?"

Because of Josh, Nicole did start going to church again. Every night at ten he began coming over to her house, and they sat at the kitchen table and read from the Book of Mormon. Gradually she began to open up to him. They talked for hours at a time about anything that came to mind.

Josh did this as her friend because there seemed to be nothing left of what had once been a romance. At times to him she seemed too fragile emotionally to ever be able to sustain a serious relationship.

13

"Josh, I need you for 'show and tell' on Wednesday," Nicole said to him in late April.

"What category? Handsome hunks of the nineties?"

"Yeah, right. No, I'm giving a speech about the idea of having bands for grownups. You know, if music educators took all the adults who wished they'd been in a band in high school and formed them into a band, think of how much fun it could be. I want you to come and show how good you've become in such a short time. Please, Josh, it'll help me get an A. I already talked to my dad. It's okay with him if you miss a day of work. Actually he said they probably wouldn't be able to tell the difference."

"All right, for you I'll do it."

Even though it was April, it snowed Tuesday night. When Josh woke up early on Wednesday, it was still snowing. The highway report indicated some blowing and drifting on the interstate, but the road was still open. Josh's father recommended that he stay home, but Josh couldn't bring himself to disappoint Nicole again. He did talk to her about the weather conditions, but she thought they could make it.

They left in Josh's car at eight in the morning. The farther they went, the stronger the wind became, until finally, about thirty miles from State College, Josh had trouble seeing the road. He slowed down to fifteen miles an hour, but they still couldn't see well enough to go on. Finally he pulled into the first turnoff they came to and stopped.

"What do we do now?" Nicole asked.

"Wait it out, I guess."

Because they didn't know how long the storm would rage or how long their gas would last, they ran the engine sparingly. They listened to the radio while the car was running. The TV station Josh's father worked for also managed a local radio station, and because this was a major storm, he had gone to work early. Throughout the day he reported on the storm. At the close of one announcement, he said, "My son, Josh, and a friend of his are out in the storm, so I'd like to go over once again precautions for survival in a car during a major storm. Be sure and check the exhaust pipe every once in a while to make sure it's not covered over with snow. And open a window a tiny crack while you're running the car so you're not breathing carbon monoxide."

"Thanks, Dad," Josh said to the radio.

The wind became an angry monster that rocked the car with each gust. The blowing and drifting were so bad that at times they could not see even three feet away.

"Let's go sit in the back seat," Josh said.

Nicole gave him a weird look. "Excuse me?"

"I'm serious. We can't keep the engine running all the time, so we're going to have to huddle together for warmth and these bucket seats and the gear shift lever are really going to get in the way."

She mimicked him. " 'We have to huddle together for warmth.' C'mon, Josh. This sounds like something you would've dreamed up in high school."

"I know it does, but this time I'm serious. We're talking survival here."

She studied his face. "All right."

As long as they were rearranging things anyway, he went outside. It felt like snow bullets were being shot into his face. Holding onto the car, he made his way back to the back, unlatched the trunk, and found an emergency survival kit, a small shovel, and a blanket. His father had given him all this when he first got the car—one of the advantages of having a weatherman for a father. The wind nearly tore the trunk lid off the car before he could shut it again. He got in the back seat with Nicole.

The emergency kit had a large candle, an empty peach can to hold it, and a large chocolate candy bar.

"Hmmm . . . chocolate," she said with a smile.

"Don't eat it all at once. This may have to last for a couple of days."

"Whatever you say."

"Now we need to get real close to conserve heat."

She leaned back against him, and he wrapped his arms around her. "This is the part you like best about a blizzard, isn't it?" she teased.

"Well, yeah." He wrapped the blanket around them.

"This is lot like camp except there's no campfire. You want to sing songs?" she asked.

"Sure."

They sang a couple of songs. "I wish Richard were here," he said. "He loved to sing. And when Richard sang, the entire county knew it."

"How can you do that?" she asked.

"What?"

"Talk about him."

"He's never left me—I just can't see him. That's the way I think of it. I felt him with me sometimes on my mission. Not supernatural . . . just a comforting feeling I had."

The next time they ran the car and listened to the radio, they found out that the interstate had been closed and all highway crews had been called in until the storm died down.

"I guess that means we're on our own," he said.

"We're going to be okay, aren't we?" she asked, sounding a little worried.

"Yeah, sure. I mean, after all, I am the son of a meteorologist."

"So?"

"I have weather genes," he boasted.

"Weather genes! Of course! Why didn't I think of that? I can see I have nothing to worry about now."

"You don't believe me, do you?"

"Oh, c'mon, Josh. When have I ever believed you?"

"Okay, that's it. This calls for drastic action."

"What?"

"I'm going to start calling you Nikki."

"I hate that name."

He used his dumb male athlete voice. "Hey, Nikki, how's it going?"

She reached for the door as if she were leaving. "That's it for me," she said.

"Okay, okay, you win." He paused. "There is one thing I'd like to do, though, while we're just hanging out here."

"What?"

"Let me look at your face."

"And let you find all the flaws? No thanks."

"There are no flaws."

"Yeah, right," she scoffed.

"C'mon, please."

"Okay, what do I have to do?"

"Just let me look at you."

"Can I look at you too?"

"If you want to."

They looked into each other's eyes for a long time and then she asked softly, "Josh, what are you thinking about?"

“How much I care about you. What are you thinking about?”

“Don’t get mad, okay? The thing I was thinking about is . . . do you know where the nearest rest room is?”

He burst out laughing. “Man, talk about destroying a mood!”

“I’m sorry, really. It’s just that this is . . . uhh . . . really important to me right now.”

They worked out an arrangement that was mutually satisfactory. It involved having him go as far away from the car as he dared to get until she called him back.

Their candy bar was marked into twenty-four squares. They decided not to eat more than one square each every hour.

The blizzard continued to rage and the temperature dropped as night came on. Even though they ran the engine part of the time, held the lighted candle next to them, and huddled together as close as they could get, they felt the numbing chill.

“I’m cold, Josh. Anything you can do about that?”

He thought about it. “Where’s your book bag?”

She leaned over into the front seat and retrieved it. As he pulled everything out, he found a neatly typed report. “What’s this?” he asked.

“It’s the paper I wrote to go with my speech. You want me to read it to you?”

“Not exactly.” He took the first page and crumpled it into a ball.

“What are you doing?” she protested.

“Stuff this inside your coat. This is insulation. We need to increase your R-factor.”

“We need to increase your R-factor,” she mimicked. “You sound just like my dad.”

He crumpled up every loose piece of paper he could find and then grabbed one of her textbooks.

"No, absolutely not! I mean it, Josh."

"I'll buy you a new book when we get out of here."

"You just don't value education, do you?"

"Part of being educated means knowing how to survive."

He ripped and crumpled the entire book. She stuffed the crumpled sheets of paper into her coat and jeans and shoes. It seemed like a crazy idea, but a while later she told him she was feeling warmer. "You always make things better for me, don't you?" she said.

It was for both of them a loaded question. "Not always," he said.

"No, not always."

"What if I had come back for Richard's funeral? How long would you have wanted me to stay?"

"I had in mind asking you not to ever go back."

"I wondered if that might happen. For me it was the toughest decision of my life. If I quit in the middle of my mission, I knew I'd disappoint Heavenly Father. But if I didn't quit, I'd disappoint you."

"You did the right thing."

"Nicole, I'll always love you."

"I know you will. That's what's makes it so hard for me, Josh—to think of leaving you and going to New York."

"Don't go. I need you here with me."

"This is hard for me to deal with because when I needed you, you didn't come. Sometimes I think my leaving is my way of punishing you."

"If you'll have me," he said, "I promise I'll never leave you again."

"If it keeps snowing like this, neither one of us is ever going to leave the other. They'll find us next July under a snowdrift, still in each other's arms."

"With a smile on our faces," he said.

A few minutes later Josh tried to get out of the car so

he could kick snow away from the exhaust pipe, but the snow was so deep he couldn't even open the door. "We can't run the engine anymore," he said.

"Why not?"

"Carbon monoxide would back up into the car. I'm just going to have to hold you closer."

"With all this paper," she said, "it must be like hugging the Pillsbury Dough Boy."

"I'm not complaining."

"I knew you wouldn't. You know, being stuffed like this makes me wonder how big I'll be when I'm going to have a baby." She sighed. "One of my big regrets is that Richard never got to be an uncle."

"He's probably everybody's uncle in the spirit world."

"I'm sure with him there, things'll never be the same. I wouldn't be surprised if they decided to rush the Second Coming just to get him out of there and resurrected." She started laughing and then suddenly stopped. "I must be getting better," she said. "At least I can talk about him now."

They huddled together, sleeping off and on, as the storm raged through the night. Once Nicole whispered, "Josh, are you awake?"

"What's wrong?"

"I think the car's completely buried in the snow. I'm afraid we're going to suffocate."

Josh crawled into the front seat, rolled down the window, and thrust his fist into the snow several times. "There's still over a foot to go before the car is completely buried," he reported.

"I'm really getting worried. Come and hold me."

He crawled into the back seat and held her in his arms.

"Sometimes I wake up late at night," she said, "and I can't get back to sleep because of missing Richard so much. Why did he have to die, Josh? I just don't understand it. Oh, Josh, I miss him so much."

"I know. Me too."

"He was so good to people. Always. He never talked bad about anyone. I know that some people think we should be glad he's dead because to them he was like a burden. There were some things he wasn't good at, but there were plenty of things he was better at than anyone else. When I came home from school, he'd be there to give me a hug and ask me how I was. And now he's not around anymore when I come home, and there's this huge vacuum in my life that's never going to get filled, and I don't know what to do about it. It's not fair. It's just not fair."

He held her and rocked her gently back and forth like a little child. "I don't know, Nicole. We might not ever know until we get on the other side."

"You were always good to him. He loved you like a brother." She paused, then said, "Josh, you know I've never loved anyone else but you, don't you?"

"Yeah, I guess I know that."

"I want you to know that, just in case we don't get out of here."

"We'll get out of here."

"If we don't though, it'll be okay, because I'll be with you, and we'll both get to see Richard."

"It's not time for us to go yet."

By four in the morning the wind died down. They fell asleep and didn't wake up until eight o'clock. Josh fought his way out of the car and looked around. Everywhere he looked the world was white and pure and beautiful. The sun on his face felt warm, though the air was still cold. He shoveled out around the car, then ran the engine because there was no need to conserve fuel anymore. The storm was over.

After he shoveled off the hood of the car, they spread out the blanket and sat on the hood and ate what was left of their chocolate. Around ten o'clock they could hear the low grumble of a road grader heading their way. Just before it came into view, Nicole wrapped her arms around him and gave him a kiss.

"What was that for?" he asked.

"That's for looking out for me."

"No problem." He paused, then asked, "Who's going to look out for you when you're in New York?"

"I'm not going to New York," she announced.

"You're not?"

"No. I'm staying here with you."

"You don't have to. I can move to New York."

"And do what?"

"I don't know. Get a job, I guess. Maybe get a basketball scholarship to Juilliard."

"Yeah, right. Cameron told me all about what you said. Look, Josh, I'll tell you the truth. I was never that crazy about going to Juilliard."

"Why not?"

"Because they mostly concentrate on performing, and lately I've decided that what I really want to do is be a band director in an elementary school someday." She looked at him curiously. "What do you want to do when you grow up?"

"Learn as much as I can from your dad about building houses and then start out on my own."

"Looks like we both know what we want, doesn't it?"

"Yeah, looks that way." He paused, then said, "Nicole, I don't know quite how to say this, but you're the only girl I've ever loved. I can't stand the thought of not being with you all the time. I don't know if this is the right time to say this, but I'm asking you to marry me in the temple. You don't have to give me an answer right away. Take your time if you want to think about it."

"Josh, are you sure? This could be either sleep deprivation or too much chocolate talking."

"I don't think so. I've always loved you and I always will."

"But I'm not the same as I was before your mission."

"I'm not either."

"I'm not sure I even belong in the temple. Right after Richard died, I spent so much time being angry with God for taking Richard that I'm not sure he'd even want me in his house."

"How are things between you and Heavenly Father now?"

"Better, but not perfect."

"I can wait until you're ready to go to the temple."

They sat on the hood of the car and talked about when they would get married and also about apartments and schooling and budgets and their honeymoon. And then he said, "This isn't exactly on the subject, but I've got to say it because it's driving me crazy."

"What?"

"You've got a little tiny smudge of chocolate on your cheek."

Her hand went to her face. "Where?"

"Stop, don't wipe it off."

She looked confused. "Why not?"

"I'm so hungry now—would it be okay with you if I just licked it off?"

She stood on the hood of the car. "All right, Dutton, that's it! You've gone too far this time!" She grabbed some snow and threw it at him.

He wasn't going to take that sitting down.

The road crew could not believe the two crazy college students having a snowball fight in the middle of the turnoff area when they showed up to rescue them.

"You're here already?" Nicole asked. "We were just starting to have fun."

A few months later Josh and Nicole were married in the Chicago Temple. The next morning they flew to Los Angeles, rented a car, and drove to Disneyland for their honeymoon. Before they got out of the car, they had a prayer to dedicate the day to Richard's memory.

"How is this going to be any different from any other tourist spending the day at Disneyland?" Josh asked.

"It doesn't have to be different," she said. "We should have a fun time, but we should also try to imagine what it would be like if Richard were here with us."

"I know one thing that would happen if Richard were with us," he said. "He'd talk to the people in line with him and make friends with them."

"We need to do that too then," she said.

They rode rides all morning and then ate lunch at the restaurant at the Pirates of the Caribbean attraction. Josh studied Nicole's face as she looked at each boatload of people moving through the darkness of the artificial night. He knew she was missing Richard.

"He would have loved it here," he said.

"I know," she said, wiping a tear from her cheek. "I've missed him so much. I tried to cover it up, but that was wrong. I was trying to avoid facing my grief. Now I know that no matter how bad it seems, you have to mourn the loss of someone you love who dies. Right now I feel as though he's here with us."

No one watching them could possibly tell any difference between them and any other tourist going to Disneyland for the first time. The things that turned this visit into a memorial for Richard were subtle. As they stood in line they made it a point to talk to the people around them, finding out where they were from and what rides they'd been on. They rode Space Mountain three times even though Nicole, by herself, would have avoided it. She screamed the entire time. They both knew that Richard would have loved that. Then they had supper at a Mexican restaurant, and while they waited for their food, they talked to the people at an adjoining table, because that is what Richard would have done.

Just before the fireworks demonstration later that night, they struck up a conversation with a family from Michigan. The woman asked, "You folks here for a vacation?"

"No, we came down to show her brother around," Josh said.

"Did he have a good time?" the stranger asked.

"Yes," Nicole reflected. "He had a great time."

Books by Jack Weyland

Brenda at the Prom

Charly

First Day of Forever

If Talent Were Pizza, You'd Be a Supreme

Kimberly

Last of the Big-time Spenders

Michelle and Debra

A New Dawn

Nicole

PepperTide

Punch and Cookies Forever

The Reunion

Sam

Sara, Whenever I Hear Your Name

A Small Light in the Darkness

Stephanie

The Understudy